PUFFIN BOOKS

The Fourth Young Puffin ⟶ ⟶ ⟶ ⟶

Barbara Ireson was born in Eastbourne. Her hobbies include restoring old houses, collecting antiques and exploring France. Barbara is one of the best regarded anthologists for children. Her first collections were made over thirty years ago and are still in print. She has since compiled many successful and popular children's verse and story collections, several of which are in Puffin.

She is married to Clifford Ireson, Emeritus Professor of Modern French Literature. They now live in Vouvray, France, where Barbara is pursuing her writing as well as helping her two sons with their antiques business.

Other collections by Barbara Ireson

The First Young Puffin Book of Bedtime Stories
The Second Young Puffin Book of Bedtime Stories
The Third Young Puffin Book of Bedtime Stories

Verse

The Young Puffin Book of Verse

For older readers

Fighting in Break and Other Stories
Haunting Tales
In a Class of Their Own

The Fourth Young Puffin Book of Bedtime Stories

Chosen by Barbara Ireson

Illustrated by Glenys Ambrus
and Caroline Sharpe

PUFFIN BOOKS

PUFFIN BOOKS

Published by the Penguin Group
Penguin Books Ltd, 27 Wrights Lane, London W8 5TZ, England
Penguin Books USA Inc., 375 Hudson Street, New York, New York 10014, USA
Penguin Books Australia Ltd, Ringwood, Victoria, Australia
Penguin Books Canada Ltd, 10 Alcorn Avenue, Toronto, Ontario, Canada M4V 3B2
Penguin Books (NZ) Ltd, 182–190 Wairau Road, Auckland 10, New Zealand

Penguin Books Ltd, Registered Offices: Harmondsworth, Middlesex, England

The stories in this collection were first published in *Story Chest: 100 Bedtime Stories* by
Viking Kestrel 1986
Published in *The Runaway Shoes* in Puffin 1989
This collection published in Puffin 1995
10 9 8 7 6 5 4 3 2

The acknowledgements on pp 149–150 constitute an extension of this copyright page

Illustrations on pages 12, 13, 15, 21, 23, 24, 26, 29, 30, 32, 36, 53, 54, 55, 57, 58, 59, 62,
66, 67, 70, 71, 73, 79, 83, 86, 88, 93, 96, 98, 116, 118, 119, 120, 123, 125, 126, 127,
138, 142, 143 copyright © Glenys Ambrus, 1986
Illustrations on pages 8, 10, 44, 45, 47, 48, 50, 52, 104, 106, 108, 109, 111, 112, 113,
114, 130, 131, 134, 135 copyright © Caroline Sharpe, 1986

Filmset in Photina

Made and printed in England by Clays Ltd, St Ives plc

CONTENTS

GOOSE FEATHERS

Of course, Debby was only eight years old. It was not surprising that she thought a skunk was a black and white kitten. But Tim was nine and three-quarters and there were things happening to him too. It was that way with the feathers. It was that way with the hundreds of goose feathers that Mrs Wiggin had stored in the feather house.

'Now that the new teacher is coming here to live we must have some new pillows,' said Mrs Wiggin. 'We must make some new pillows for the four-poster bed.'

'Oh, she doesn't need pillows,' said Tim.

But they all went into the feather house and closed the door. Piles of fluffy white feathers lay on the table.

'Here are the pillow tickings,' said Mrs Wiggin. 'We'll stuff them full of feathers.'

'For the teacher,' said Debby.

'Aw,' said Tim. 'I hope they're hard.'

Mrs Wiggin scooped up handfuls of feathers. She put them into the tick that Tim held for her. Debby was clapping her hands to make the feathers skip about. When she giggled, a cloud of them would flutter up. It took only a breath of air to move them. They sailed lightly up and then floated down again on the table.

'The baby's crying,' said Tim.

'Oh, dear,' said his mother. 'I was hoping she would sleep until we finished these. I'll have to go and feed her. You hold this, Debby, and Tim can put the feathers in. I'll be back in a few minutes. If you go out, be sure to close the door behind you.'

'Yes,' said Tim.

He stuffed the feathers in. He pushed them in fast to make the pillow as hard as he could. It couldn't be too hard for that teacher, he thought.

'Hold it straight, Debby,' he said.

'My arms ache,' said Debby. 'They ache up into my neck.'

'Rest your arms on the table. Hold the bag wide open,' Tim said.

'Oh, ouch, ouch!' squealed Debby. 'There's a feather tickling my nose. Take it off.'

'Hold still, Debby. Blow it off yourself.'

'Oh, ouch!' she squealed. 'It won't go.'

'Hold still!' cried Tim. 'You're stirring all the feathers up.'

'Oh, ouch!' cried Debby.

She wriggled and kicked. She waved the pillow tick around her head. She made a big wind with the pillow tick. The feathers swirled about.

'They're all over me! Take them off, Tim. Take them off. They tickle!'

The feather house was full of floating feathers. They were like a snowstorm.

'Stop it. Stop it!' cried Tim, and he tried to catch Debby.

'Let me go!' she screamed. 'Let me go!'

She jerked away from Tim. She opened the door and ran out.

'Come back with that sack,' called Tim, and he ran out of the feather house after her.

They ran past the woodshed and into the potato field. The feathers flew off Debby as she ran. Half-way across the field Tim caught her.

'Give me that sack,' he cried.

But the pillow tick flew up in the air and out of it floated a cloud of feathers. There was a strong breeze blowing and off went the feathers towards the woods.

Debby watched them as long as she could see them.

'There go some of the teacher's feathers,' she said.

'You're a bad girl,' said Tim. 'Now there won't be enough to make the pillows too hard.'

'Tim! Timothy Wiggin!'

It was his mother calling. Tim and Debby looked towards the house.

'Why, it's snowing,' said Debby. 'Look! It's snowing hard.'

But Tim's heart jumped so high that it almost went out through the top of his head. He began to run across the potato field as fast as he could. Mrs Wiggin was running towards the feather house. Great flakes of snow were floating from the open door.

Tim had left the door open! The feathers were drifting like snow across the yard and into the apple orchard. They were drifting like a blizzard into the apple orchard.

Mrs Wiggin stood with the baby under her arm. She was looking into the empty feather house. Tim stood looking in too. And Debby. There were about six feathers left in it.

Then they all turned and watched the feathers. They sifted past the house and past the little apple trees. Some of them hung in the apple trees. They hung in the apple trees like apple blossoms. But most of them floated away on the breeze.

'There go two good pillows,' Mrs Wiggin said at last. 'Two good big pillows. Something always happens, seems so to me, seems so.'

Tim said nothing.

And Debby said nothing too.

The feathers flew around all the evening. They fluttered up and they fluttered down. Mr Wiggin came back from the woods with feathers in his hair. Sarah, the cow, wore a crown of them between her horns. Trot, the dog, chased them. He thought they were

butterflies. The pigs snuffed and grunted. The feathers stuck to their noses. The geese looked surprised. Were they losing their feathers again?

Only the birds were happy. They scurried and hurried about. They were gathering feathers – the robins, the bobolinks, the bluebirds, and the meadowlarks. They cheeped and sang as they gathered the feathers to line their nests.

All the birds had warm feather beds that summer, but there were no new pillows for the four-poster bed.

'Accidents will happen, seems so to me, seems so,' said Mr Wiggin.

'Yes, they do in this topsy-turvy family,' Mrs Wiggin said. 'But we can put the children's pillows in the front room.'

'Oh, yes!' cried Debby. 'Then the teacher won't have to be without any.'

'Aw!' said Tim. 'Why do we have to have a teacher?'

EMMA L. BROCK

SILLY BILLY

Little White Goat lived on a farm with lots of other goats. He was always getting into mischief, leaving the herd of goats and wandering off on his own. Then he would get into trouble. The farmer's wife was always having to search for him among the farm buildings where Little Goat would hide.

She told her husband, 'That silly little goat is always in trouble. He won't stay with the other goats and I never know where to find him. Yesterday, I found him chasing the chickens – then he followed me into the kitchen and started eating the tablecloth – he nearly pulled it off, then all my dishes would have been broken. You'll have to keep him fastened up. He's nothing but a nuisance.'

The farmer laughed. 'Don't get so upset, my dear. He's young yet, but he'll settle down soon, so stop worrying.'

The next day the farmer milked the cows and put the milk churns in the dairy. Then he drove the cows into the meadow.

While he was away that naughty little goat got loose and wandered across the farmyard to the dairy. He pushed open the door and went inside.

There he saw a big bowl of cream on the table. He sniffed it – 'atchoo!' it went up his nose. Then he tasted it – it tasted so good that he drank it all up.

He looked on a shelf and found a big cheese. He reached up and began to eat it. 'Yum, yum!' He liked that better than the cream.

Then he looked around and saw the milk churns. He tried to take off the lid to look inside, but the churn tipped over, the lid came off and out splashed the milk, all over the goat and all over the floor.

Little White Goat rushed outside as the milk churn rolled and clattered after him. He slipped and slid over the river of milk as it flowed out of the dairy into the farmyard.

Little Goat dashed across the farmyard scattering the hens and chickens. They set up such a squawking and cackling that the farmer's wife came out to see what all the noise was about.

11

When she saw Little White Goat she was very angry. 'What have you done, you silly-billy? Be off with you!'

She picked up a broom and chased him away. Then she went into the dairy to clear up the mess.

When the farmer came home she had such a tale to tell.

'That silly goat has been in trouble again. He got into the dairy, drank the cream, ate the cheese and upset a churn of milk all over the floor. I've been clearing up all day. I'm tired of that troublesome goat, he'll have to go. Can't *you* do something about him?'

'There now! Don't take on so! He's only young yet but he'll soon settle down. I'll put him in the orchard tomorrow. He'll be out of your way there,' her husband replied, trying hard to soothe her.

The next day the farmer drove Little Goat into the orchard. Then he shut the gate and spoke to him.

'Now stay there today and don't get in any more trouble. See if you can be good for a change.'

Little Goat bleated as he kicked up his heels and cantered away. The farmer went back to the farm and soon was driving his tractor into a field to start ploughing.

Silly Billy wandered around the orchard looking for mischief. There was nothing to do except eat grass and stare at the trees above him. Then he did see what he could do, for the trees were loaded with apples and some of the branches were low enough for him to reach. He stood on his hind legs and reached up. He shook the branches until the apples fell down. 'Bump, bump, bumpety bump' they tumbled down, some bumping on his head, but he didn't mind. He crunched the apples happily, although he wasn't to know that they were green and unripe and quite sour. When he was full he lay down to rest.

He did not rest long for soon he began to feel ill. He rolled over and over in agony with terrible pains in his stomach. He staggered to his feet and bleated loudly for help.

The farmer's wife was in the farmyard feeding the hens and chickens and she heard his bleating. She hurried to the orchard to find out what was the matter. When she saw Little Goat staggering about in such pain she was very sorry.

She helped him to the stable and put him to rest on some straw.

'There, there! You poor little goat, what is the matter? You look so ill and in such pain. I'll fetch my husband, he'll know what to do. I won't be long, so you rest there until I come back.'

She hurried to the field and called and called but her husband could not hear her for the noise from the tractor. Then he saw her waving frantically so he stopped the tractor and ran to her.

'What's the matter?' he asked.

'Little Goat is very ill, he was staggering around the orchard in such pain, so I put him in the stable. Do come and see him, he might die!'

They hurried to the stable and the farmer looked at Little Goat, then prodded him gently while Little Goat bleated plaintively.

13

'He's certainly in pain and I know why. I ought to have known better. I should never have put him in the orchard. He's been eating sour unripe apples, that's why he is ill. He has colic.'

'But he couldn't reach them,' said his wife.

'You don't know goats, my dear. If they want something to eat they'll find a way of getting it. Perhaps this will teach him a lesson. I'll give him a dose of medicine to stop the pain. He'll be all right tomorrow, you'll see.'

Sure enough Little Goat was better the next day and was allowed out in the farmyard. He was very quiet and didn't even chase the chickens. The farmer's wife was very pleased and told her husband.

'Little Goat has been very good today. He's followed me around quietly all day long. Perhaps he won't get into any more trouble.'

She was wrong!

The next day was wash day and she hung all her washing on the line. Soon it was blowing in the breeze.

The farmer came towards her leading Little Goat and carrying a rope in his hand.

'What are you going to do?' she asked.

'I'm going to make sure that Little Goat is safe today. I'll fasten him to the tree on the lawn. Then he can't wander away and get into trouble.'

'Good! I can get on with my work now,' said his wife and she went indoors while the farmer went off to the field in his tractor.

Little Goat walked round and round the tree until he felt quite dizzy. Then he ate some of the juicy, green grass. Then he looked around – and guess what he saw! A lovely line of washing, blowing in the breeze! He wished he was free to go and look at it. Suddenly he had a clever idea. He nibbled and gnawed at the rope which tied him to the tree, and soon he was free. He certainly was a clever, inquisitive, mischievous goat, for he walked very quietly across the grass to the washing line. Then he knocked down the wooden prop which held the line high, so now he could reach the washing easily.

He fancied a pair of red socks and began to eat them. 'Yum, yum!' They tasted very good. Then he nibbled delicately at a towel – mmm, quite tasty! But what was on the rest of the menu? A bright blue striped shirt! He began to chew that. Ah! this tasted best of

all, so he ate big holes in it. He was so busy eating he did not hear the farmer's wife come out to fetch her washing.

When she saw the goat she went *mad*! She grabbed a broom and chased him.

'Get away from my washing, you scoundrel! Look what you've done! This is the last straw – you'll have to go!' She chased him round the farmyard while the hens and chickens squawked in terror as they tried to get out of the way. At last she chased him into the stable and shut the door.

'Stay there! *You*'ll be in trouble when I tell my husband what you've done,' she panted breathlessly.

When the farmer came back from the fields, she met him at the gate.

'Wait till I tell you what that silly goat has been up to today.'

'But I tied him up this morning, so how could he be in trouble again?' he asked.

'I'll tell you how. He got loose from the rope, then he went to my washing line and ate your socks, made holes in my best towel and ruined your blue striped shirt. He ate so much of it that it's only fit for a duster now. He bit through the rope – that's how he got loose.'

'Where is he now?' asked the farmer.

'In the stable. You'll have to get rid of him. Take him to market and sell him, for I'm fed up with him.'

'Now, now! Don't take on so. It isn't the end of the world, you know. He's only young and full of mischief. He'll settle down soon – you'll see! Tomorrow he can go with the big goats. He won't be able to get out of that field, I'll make sure of that.' The farmer sighed as he put away the tractor and went indoors.

Next day Little Goat was taken to the field away from the farm and stayed there with the big goats. He liked it there for he could roam around and eat the juicy green grass.

After a while he became restless and wandered away from the big goats and came to the far end of the field. There he managed to squeeze through a gap in the hedge – and he was out on the open road.

'Oh this is great fun,' he thought as he clip-clopped along the road. Suddenly he heard a loud noise – he turned and saw a big milk lorry rushing towards him. He leapt to the roadside just in time. That scared him so he kept to the side of the road where he was safe.

Soon he came to a busy main road. He looked around him, bewildered by all the noise; cars, lorries and buses were whizzing by, making him terrified. He tried to get away, dodging in and out of the traffic. Drivers slammed on their brakes and stopped as Little Goat stood bleating with fright, in the middle of the traffic jam.

A police car drove up and stopped while a policeman jumped out to see what was the matter. 'What's going on here? Who's blocking the road?' he asked.

One of the motorists laughed and answered,

'You might ask that silly goat standing in the middle of the road – he's the culprit!'

The policeman hurried towards the goat and grabbed hold of him. Silly Little Goat was only too glad to be taken away from the traffic.

The drivers laughed and one asked, 'Are you arresting the goat, Constable?'

The policeman saw the funny side of the problem. 'Yes!' he answered. 'I'm taking him into custody for obstructing the traffic.'

By this time the second policeman had joined them. He directed the traffic and soon the road was clear.

'What are we going to do with him?' he asked as they walked back to the car.

'Get the tow rope from the boot of the car and we'll fasten the goat to the back bumper.'

Soon they were driving slowly along the road with Silly Billy trailing behind them.

People stared and laughed when they saw the goat, and the children became very excited to see such a funny sight. They followed on the pavement, keeping up with the car, for they wanted to see where the police were taking him.

At last they reached the police station. The goat was untied and taken inside while one policeman stayed outside and explained what had happened, as the children clamoured to know all about it.

As for the goat, he was put in a cell and locked up until the police could find his owner.

Back at the farm at the end of the day the farmer went to drive the goats back to the farm. He looked for Little Goat; he searched all over the field and came to the gap in the hedge. Then he knew where Little Goat had gone – he had run away!

He hurried back to the farm, driving the goats in front of him. Then he called to his wife as he went indoors.

'Little Goat has run away. I'll have to go and look for him before it's dark.'

'Wait a minute!' his wife answered. 'Don't go yet. Why don't you ring up the police first? They may know something – someone may have found him and reported it to the police.'

'All right! I'll fasten the goats up for the night and then ring up,' he answered.

Soon he was back and picked up the phone and asked for the police.

'Has anyone reported finding a little white goat, because I've lost one? What's that? You've got one locked up in a cell ... He's what? He's trying to knock the door down! ... All right – I'll come right over ... Yes! I'll bring my truck. Thank you very much.'

'What did they say?' asked his wife.

'It's all right, my dear, don't worry. Little Goat is safe. They've locked him up in a police cell. I'll fetch him at once before he kicks the door down – I won't be long.'

Off went the farmer with his truck and soon arrived at the police station. As soon as Little Goat saw him he quietened down. He was led out of the cell and put in the truck.

'Make sure you keep him off the roads in future. He could have caused a nasty accident, or got killed,' said the policeman as they fastened the goat securely in the truck.

'I'll make sure of that – don't worry,' answered the farmer. 'Thank you very much for looking after him.'

As they drove away Little Goat was very quiet. This time he had really learned his lesson. He did not want to get run over. He did not want to be locked up in a police cell ever again. All he wanted was to get safely back home to the farm.

So, at last Little Goat had grown up and he never, never got into trouble again.

GLADYS LEES

THE PAGE BOY AND THE SILVER GOBLET

There was once a little page boy who was in service in a stately castle on the Scottish west coast. He was a pleasant, good-natured little fellow and carried out his duties so willingly that he was popular with everyone, including the great earl whom he served

18

every day and the fat old butler for whom he ran errands. The castle stood on the edge of a cliff overlooking the sea and although the walls on that side were very thick, there was a small postern door which allowed only one person to pass through to a narrow flight of steps cut out of the cliff side and leading down to the seashore. The shore was a pleasant place on summer mornings when one could bathe in the shimmering sea.

On the other side of the castle were gardens and pleasure grounds opening on to a long stretch of heather-covered moorland and beyond was a chain of lofty mountains. The little page boy was very fond of going out on the moor when his work was done. He could then run about as much as he liked, chasing bumblebees, catching butterflies, looking for birds' nests when it was nesting time and watching the young birds learning to fly.

The old butler was very pleased that he should go out on the moor for he knew that it was good for a healthy little lad to have plenty of fun in the open air. But before the boy went out the old man always gave him one warning. 'Now, mind my words, laddie, and keep away from the fairy knowe on the moor, for the little folk are not to be trusted.'

This knowe of which he spoke was a little green hillock which stood on the moor about fifty yards from the garden gate and the local people said that it was the abode of the fairies who would punish any rash mortal who went too near them. It was also known as Boot Hill and according to the great earl the hillock had been made hundreds of years before when visiting noblemen cleaned the earth and mud from their boots on the hill before entering the castle. Because of the various stories the country folk would walk a good half mile out of their way, even in broad daylight, rather than run the risk of going near the hillock and bringing the little folk's displeasure down upon themselves. At night, they said, the fairies walked abroad, leaving the door of their dwelling open so that any foolish mortal who did not take care might find himself inside.

Now, the little page boy was an adventurous lad, and instead of being frightened of the fairies he was very anxious to see them and visit their abode, just to find out what it was like. One night, when everyone else was asleep, he crept out of the castle by the little postern door and stole down the steps, then along the seashore to a path leading up on to the moor.

He went straight to the fairy knowe and to his delight he found that what the local people had said was true. The top of the knowe was tipped up and from the opening came rays of light streaming into the darkness. His heart was beating fast with excitement, but gathering his courage he stooped down and slipped inside. He found himself in a large room lit by numberless tiny candles and there, seated round a polished marble table, were scores of tiny folk: fairies, elves and gnomes, dressed in green, yellow, pink, blue, lilac and scarlet; in fact, all the colours of the rainbow.

The little page boy stood in a dark corner watching the busy scene in wonder, thinking how strange it was that there should be such a number of those tiny beings living their own lives all unknown to men and yet not far away from human dwellings. Suddenly an order was given, by whom he could not tell.

'Fetch the cup,' cried the unknown voice and instantly two little fairy pages dressed in scarlet darted from the table to a cupboard in the wall of the compartment. They returned staggering under the weight of a most beautiful silver goblet, richly embossed and lined inside with gold.

The silver cup was placed on the middle of the table and, amid clapping of hands and shouts of joy, all the fairies began to drink out of it in turn. The page boy could see from where he stood that no one poured wine into the cup and yet it appeared to be always full. The wine that was in it was not always of the same kind, but sometimes red and sometimes white. Each fairy, when he grasped the stem, wished for the wine he desired, and lo, in a moment the cup was full of it. 'It would be a fine thing if I could take that cup home with me,' thought the page boy. 'No one will believe that I have been here unless I have something to show for it.' So he bided his time and waited.

Presently the fairies noticed him and, instead of being angry at his boldness in entering their abode, as he expected, they seemed very pleased to see him and invited him to take a seat at the table. But not long after he sat down they became rude and insolent, whispering together and peering at him and asking why he should be content to serve mere mortals. They also told him that they were aware of everything that went on in the castle and made fun of the old butler whom the page boy loved. They laughed at the food served in the castle and said it was only fit for animals. When any fresh, dainty food was set on the table by the scarlet-clad fairy pages they would push the dish across to him saying: 'Taste it, for you will not have the chance to taste such good things at the castle.'

At last, he could stand their teasing remarks no longer; besides, he knew that if he wanted to secure the silver cup he must not lose any more time in doing so as they all appeared to be turning against him. Suddenly he stood up and grabbed the cup from the table, holding the stem of it lightly in his hand.

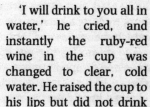

'I will drink to you all in water,' he cried, and instantly the ruby-red wine in the cup was changed to clear, cold water. He raised the cup to his lips but did not drink from it. With a sudden jerk he threw the water over the burning candles and instantly the room was in darkness. Then, clasping the precious cup tightly in his arms, he sprang to the opening of the knowe through which he could see the stars gleaming clearly in the sky. He was just in time, for the opening like a trap door fell with a crash behind him. Soon he was speeding along the moor with the whole troop of fairies at his heels. They were wild with rage and from the shrill shouts of fury the page

21

boy knew that if they overtook him he could expect no mercy at their hands.

The page boy's heart began to sink, for fleet of foot though he was, he was no match for the fairy folk who were steadily gaining on him. All seemed lost, when a mysterious voice sounded out of the darkness:

> *If you would gain the castle door,*
> *Keep to the black stones on the shore.*

It was the voice of some poor mortal, who, for some reason or other, had been taken prisoner by the fairies and who did not want such a fate to befall the adventurous page boy; but the little fellow did not know this. He had once heard that if one walked on the wet sands which the waves had washed over the fairies could not touch him. The mysterious voice brought the saying into his mind. He dashed panting down the path to the shore, his feet sank into the dry sand and his breath came in little gasps. He felt as if he must drop the silver cup and give up the struggle, but he persevered and at last, just as the foremost fairies were about to lay hands on him, he jumped across the water mark on to firm, wet sand from which the waves had just receded. He was now safe. The little folk could go no further but stood on the dry sand uttering cries of rage and disappointment while the page boy ran triumphantly by the edge of the sea carrying the precious cup in his arms. He climbed lightly up the steps in the rock and disappeared through the postern door into the castle.

For many years afterwards, long after the little page boy had grown up and had become a stately butler who trained other little page boys to follow in his footsteps, the beautiful goblet remained in the castle as a witness to his adventure.

GRANT CAMPBELL

THE TERRIBLY PLAIN PRINCESS

Once upon a time there was this terribly plain Princess. I won't beat about the bush – she was terribly plain. All the visitors at the Royal Christening remarked upon it.

'How extraordinarily plain she is,' said her aunt as she handed over a solid silver spoon as a christening present.

'Quite exceptionally so,' said her cousin-once-removed as she put a solid gold napkin ring into the Princess's tiny hands.

I say tiny hands, but her hands were a great deal larger than those of most Royal Princesses. Her mouth was wider, too, and her nose was hopelessly snubbed. She also had twenty-three freckles over her nose and cheeks.

The King and Queen watched anxiously as the pile of presents grew higher and the comments on the Princess's plainness grew franker. Finally, the Lord High Chamberlain presented the child with a portrait of himself wearing his full robes of office.

'We shall be hard put to find her a husband,' he said gloomily, shaking his head with the worry of it all. The poor Queen could bear it no longer. She burst into tears and sobbed all over the King's best ermine cloak, which did it no good.

The Princess, whose name was Sophia, lived on an island with her mother, Good Queen Matilda, and her father, Good King Ferdinand. The island was the Island of Toow and was one of a group of islands with original names like the Island of Wun and the Island of Thri. Further over to the right was the Island of Faw but nobody talked about that one. It was uninhabited and a bit of an eyesore with trees and wild flowers all over the place and no street lighting. All the islands were surrounded by seas of an incredible blue and a golden sun shone all the time.

The terribly plain Princess thrived in this beautiful kingdom,

but any hopes that she might grow out of her plainness faded with the passing of the years. She didn't look like a Princess and she didn't behave like one. Sometimes her Royal cousins from Thri and Wun would come over to visit.

They would play very genteel games like 'The farmer's in his Royal den,' and 'Here we go gathering Royal nuts in May,' but the Princess Sophia was bored by it all. She would slip away to find Bert, the gardener's boy. He was her one and only true best friend in all the world – or so she told him.

Bert was also terribly plain. He had a snub nose, large hands, a wide mouth and twenty-eight freckles. He worked very hard because the gardener was bone idle and spent most of his time sleeping in a wheelbarrow in the shade of a Royal pear tree.

Bert trimmed the hedges, and weeded the paths and raked the leaves off the grass. When Bert wasn't working in the gardens he was busy with his secret plan to grow a giant blue marigold. He confided this secret to no one but the Princess Sophia – and the cook and most of his relations (and he came from a very large family).

The Princess loved to help him, and together they mixed powders to sprinkle and solutions to spray. They grew a giant orange marigold and some small blue marigolds but never a giant blue one. It was very disappointing for Bert but he was a sunny sort of boy and he refused to give up hope.

When the terribly plain Princess was fifteen, Good King Ferdinand sent for the Lord High Chamberlain.

'Look here,' he said, 'what are you doing about finding a husband for the Princess Sophia?'

The Lord High Chamberlain bowed low.

'Everything is in hand, Your Majesty,' he said proudly. 'I think I may say in all modesty, and without fear of contradiction, though I say it myself as shouldn't –'

'Get on with it, man,' said the King. It was rather unkingly of him but his nerves were frayed by sleepless nights spent worrying about his daughter's future.

The Lord High Chamberlain tried again. 'Bearing in mind the Princess Sophia's terrible plainness of face and largeness of hands, I have now discovered the ideal husband for your daughter.'

The King sighed.

'I suppose he, too, is terribly plain,' he said.

'On the contrary, Your Majesty, Prince Archibald is of Royal and noble countenance.'

The King began to feel much happier.

'And where does this Prince live?' he asked.

'On the Island of Ayte,' said the Lord High Chamberlain.

The King lowered his voice to a whisper.

'And what is it that makes the Prince an ideal husband for the Princess Sophia?' he asked.

The Lord High Chamberlain lowered his voice also.

'Your Majesty,' he said, 'the Prince Archibald is terribly short-sighted – in a Royal sort of way. I doubt if he will notice that his bride is terribly plain.'

Good King Ferdinand was delighted. He told Good Queen Matilda who was delighted and together they told the Princess Sophia who was horrified.

'But I don't want to marry him,' she protested and she stamped her foot and looked plainer than ever. 'I want to marry Bert, the gardener's boy, and help him grow a giant blue marigold.'

'But dearest child,' said her mother. 'The gardener's boy is terribly plain and Prince Archibald is of Royal and noble countenance.'

'Royal and noble poppycock!' said the Princess. 'I want to marry Bert.'

But her protestations went unheeded and the date was set for the wedding. You may well be wondering what Bert had to say about all this. The fact is that he didn't say anything because he had designed a square parasol to shelter the marigolds from the sun's rays at midday and was try-ing to decide the best position for it.

On the Island of Ayte, Prince Archibald was not looking for-ward to his coming betrothal either, because he was a con-firmed bookworm. His rooms in the palace had books where books should be and books where books shouldn't be. Scattered among the books were various pairs of spectacles to help him with his reading. (There were times when his parents worried about him.)

The day of the Royal wedding dawned bright and clear. The Royal party set sail from the Island of Ayte in the Good Ship Aytee, bound for the Island of Toow.

The Princess Sophia waited on the quayside with Good King Ferdinand and Good Queen Matilda and the Lord High Chamberlain and hundreds of lesser mortals. The terribly plain Princess wore a beautiful gown of white and gold lace and a rather thick veil. As the Prince's ship drew alongside the quay a great cheer went up from the Princess's supporters and the Prince put down his book and went up on deck. It was a proud moment for the people of Toow when the Prince Archibald, of Royal and noble countenance, prepared to meet the terribly plain Princess Sophia.

But it was not to be. It so happened that the Prince Archibald had forgotten to take off his reading spectacles and put on his walking-about spectacles. Instead of stepping on to the ship's gangplank he missed it by a good few inches and stepped straight into the incredibly blue sea!

Now, although the people of Toow were nice, well-mannered people, it isn't every day you can see a Royal Prince plopping into the water like that. I have to admit that they all fell about laughing. Some of them laughed so much that *they* fell into the water as well.

Poor Prince Archibald was very upset. As soon as he was fished out of the water he gave orders to sail back to Ayte and turned to the next chapter in his book. The terribly plain Princess Sophia was also upset. She ran away to find Bert and weep on his shoulder, but when she did find him he was at the top of a step-ladder, adjusting the square parasol over his precious marigold plants. The princess fell to her knees on the grass below him, and wept terribly plain tears all over the marigold.

When Bert came down five minutes later to see what was going on he could hardly believe his eyes. The marigolds were beginning to grow! The plants grew taller and taller and produced giant

27

buds which burst into bloom. Yes! You've guessed it. Bright blue marigolds!

That's almost the end of the story. Bert was awarded a medal – the Gardener's Silver Cross – and he was allowed to marry the Princess. They went to live on the Island of Faw where they raised many new and wonderful plants with the help of Princess Sophia's terribly plain tears. (She could cry to order by thinking how nearly she had married Prince Archibald!) Oh yes! They also raised a large family of happy, but terribly plain, children!

PAMELA OLDFIELD

THE RUNAWAY SHOES

In a faraway part of the world, there is a little town called Pokey-doke. And on the edge of this town is a little red house. Mr and Mrs Nickelodeon Kumquat live there.

One day Mr and Mrs Nickelodeon Kumquat cleaned and polished their good shoes. Mrs Kumquat set them all out on the back stoop to dry. As soon as she went back inside the house, all four shoes began talking at once.

'Goody,' said the first shoe.

'Now's our chance,' said the second shoe.

'To run away,' said the third shoe.

'Let's go!' said the fourth shoe.

So they hopped down the steps and they tiptoed down the path and they walked across the lawn and they RAN across the road and into a field.

But Mr Nickelodeon Kumquat saw them go. He was looking out of a window.

'Mrs Kumquat,' he cried. 'Come quickly. Our shoes are running away. We must catch them and bring them home.'

Mr and Mrs Nickelodeon Kumquat rushed out of the house in their bedroom slippers. They jumped down the steps and they leaped down the path and they bounced across the lawn and they RAN across the road and into the field.

When the shoes saw Mr and Mrs Nickelodeon Kumquat running after them, they all began to talk at once.

'Perhaps we'd better hide,' said the first shoe.

'And wait for a while,' said the second shoe.

'Until they get past us,' said the third shoe.

'Let's run!' said the fourth shoe.

Licketysplit across the field ran the shoes. Out in the middle of the field they saw a cow.

'Oh, Cow,' said the first shoe.

'Will you do us a favour?' said the second shoe.

'Just put one shoe on each foot,' said the third shoe.

'And make believe you always wear shoes,' said the fourth shoe.

'Gladly,' said the cow. 'Moo-oo-oost gladly.'

So the cow put on the shoes and stood still, looking up at the sky and pretending to watch for the stars to come out.

As Mr and Mrs Nickelodeon Kumquat ran past the cow, Mr Kumquat shouted over his shoulder,

'Did you see any shoes run past you?'

'Not I,' said the cow. 'I didn't see any shoes run past me.' And she told the truth, too.

But just then Mrs Kumquat stopped running.

'Mr Kumquat,' she said. 'Did you ever see a cow with shoes on before?'

'Why, no,' said Mr Kumquat. 'Come to think of it, I never did. Those must be our shoes on that cow!' So they turned around and started to run back.

'Oh my!' said the first shoe.

'They're coming back!' said the second shoe.

'We didn't fool them!' said the third shoe.

'Let's run!' cried the fourth shoe.

So they said thank you politely to the cow and the four shoes ran licketysplit down to the edge of the brook. There they saw a crocodile. Don't ask me how he happened to be there. He just was.

'Oh, Crocodile,' said the first shoe.

'Will you do us a favour?' said the second shoe.

'Just put one shoe on each foot,' said the third shoe.

'And make believe you always wear shoes,' said the fourth shoe.

'Well,' said the crocodile, 'it's hardly the sort of thing I'd want to do every day in the week, but all right.'

So he put on the shoes and he stood still at the edge of the brook.

He hummed a little song his mother had taught him when he was small and he pretended he was singing himself to sleep.

As Mr and Mrs Nickelodeon Kumquat ran past the crocodile, Mr Kumquat shouted over his shoulder, 'Did you see any shoes run past you, Crocodile?'

'Not I,' said the crocodile. 'I didn't see any shoes run past me.' And he told the truth, too.

But just then, Mr Kumquat stopped running.

'Mrs Kumquat,' he said. 'Did you ever see a crocodile with shoes on before?'

'Why, no,' said Mrs Kumquat. 'Come to think of it, I never did. Those must be our shoes on that crocodile!' So they turned around and started to run back towards the crocodile.

'Oh my!' said the first shoe.

'They're coming back!' said the second shoe.

'We didn't fool them!' said the third shoe.

'Let's run!' cried the fourth shoe.

So they said thank you politely to the crocodile and the four shoes ran licketysplit right into the middle of the woods and Mr and Mrs Nickelodeon Kumquat never saw where they went. So Mr and Mrs Kumquat had to go home in their bedroom slippers.

All day long the four shoes had a wonderful time. They walked up the sides of trees and walked along the branches. They hopped into mud puddles. They floated on the brook like little boats.

In the afternoon they started off towards town. When they came to a barn, they walked up one side and over the roof and down the other side. When they came to a fence they walked on top of it. Sometimes they even walked on the telephone wires!

'It's getting late,' said the first shoe.

'We'd better go home,' said the second shoe.

'But, gosh –' said the third shoe.

'We're awfully dirty,' said the fourth shoe.

And they certainly were. They didn't look at all like the same shoes Mr and Mrs Nickelodeon Kumquat had cleaned and polished that morning.

So the four shoes walked down the main street and walked into the shoemaker's shop and hopped up on the shelf.

In a few minutes the shoemaker turned around and saw them.

'Well my goodness,' he said. 'Those shoes belong to Mr and Mrs Nickelodeon Kumquat. I mended them last month. I wonder how they got here.'

He thought for a while and then he said, 'Mr and Mrs Nickelodeon Kumquat must have left them here when I was out for lunch.'

So the shoemaker cleaned and polished the shoes until they looked brand new. Then he put them back on the shelf.

Later, when the shoemaker wasn't looking, the four shoes hopped down from the shelf and skipped up the street. They went straight back to the little red house where Mr and Mrs Kumquat live.

There they stood, lined up in a row on the steps when Mr Nickelodeon Kumquat opened the door just before suppertime.

'Mrs Kumquat,' he cried. 'Come quickly!'

Mrs Nickelodeon Kumquat came.

'Why, there are our shoes!' she said. 'Now how do you suppose they got there?'

'Well,' said Mr Nickelodeon Kumquat with a wink, 'that's just where you put them this morning, isn't it?'

And he told the truth, too.

EDNA PRESTON

THE KIDNAPPING OF LORD COCKEREL

Not very long ago, a man and his wife lived in a small flat in the centre of a noisy city. Every morning, they were woken by the sound of the milk train clattering through a nearby tunnel; every evening, there was a great blowing of horns, stamping of feet and calling of 'Paper! Paper!' by news-boys as tired people made their way home from work. For many years, they didn't bother very much about the clamour; after all, it was company. They had no children and would have been dreadfully quiet all by themselves. But one midsummer day, when they had to close their windows because of the roar of the buses and stop up their ears because of the screech of brakes, the man put down his knife and fork and pushed back his chair.

'Alice,' he said. 'I've got an idea. We'll go and live in the country.'

'In the *country*, George?' questioned his wife in surprise. A dreamy look came into her eyes. 'You mean, the *real* country? With haystacks? And pigs?'

'*Certainly* with pigs. We'll have a farm. We'll sell the flat. We'll buy a cottage. We'll have animals, and vegetables, and take things as they come, see? We'll GO.'

Then he finished up his steak-and-kidney pudding, and together they studied the railway timetable to find out when the next train might be travelling to the country. The *real* country. With pigs.

33

There was one that very afternoon.

So you see *that* was how George and Alice began. The cottage they found was dark and rickety. There were tiny windows and crooked floors, a gate that was half off its hinges, and a cellar full of cobwebs and mice. But there were outhouses, a vegetable patch, a pigsty ... and best of all, a bit of meadow land.

They worked hard, and soon had everything to rights. Little by little, they began to stock the farm.

The first animal to be bought was a cow, for they needed milk for themselves and could sell what was left over. Then a pig, and half a dozen chickens. A cat, to keep the mice away. A dog, to guard the house. And a donkey.

They hesitated a bit about the donkey, but the man said it would cost nothing to feed – it could live in the meadow and sleep in one of the outhouses. And it would be useful for carrying things to the market, when they had enough to sell.

'Cabbages ... and eggs ... and cooking apples ...' he explained. 'We shall soon build up a business. We must take things as they come.

'What's the matter?'

Alice was looking worried.

'There's one thing that bothers me,' she said. 'We'll have to get up very early to look after all these animals. There isn't a milk train here, or motor horns and the alarm clock got broken when we moved house.

'What shall we do?'

They thought. It really was a problem. They were so accustomed to noise ... with so much silence, one could almost sleep for ever. And then what would happen? What would happen if they *never* woke up?

'I have it!' George thumped the table. 'A cockerel. That's what we need. A cockerel always crows, just as dawn is breaking. That'll wake us, come what may.'

So they bought a cockerel.

What a voice he had, that cockerel! His was the loudest in the yard by far. How proud he was of it, too.

'Cock-a-doodle-doo! Wake up, you people, do!' he screamed, as the first pale glimmer of sun lighted the horizon. The other animals groaned and grunted and muttered crossly that they were busy dreaming and did not want to be disturbed. But George and Alice rolled out of bed and started mixing the chicken feed and milking the cow. There was a lot to do on a farm, and they had to begin early or they would not finish by bedtime.

To begin with, it was a happy arrangement, and all went well. But soon the animals began to be irritated by the cockerel. It was one thing being told that dawn was breaking; it was quite another to hear that loud, raucous cry so often – during one's noontime nap, when one was searching for truffles, or pulling up worms. And he was so beautiful.

'I'm smarter than you!' he would crow. 'What stupid things you do!' The cockerel strutted about among the brown hens, pushing them out of the way and helping himself to the tastiest morsels.

'I am the Lord of you all,' he announced. 'It is well known that the man and his wife cannot get out of bed without my instructions. The success of the farm depends entirely on my own efforts. You are indeed fortunate to have me among you. Why, even the sun does not rise until he has heard me! That is my cousin, up there on the church steeple. You can see that he is covered in gold; every Sunday, human beings come into the building and sing songs to him.

'They are not very good songs,' mused the cockerel critically, 'but then human beings do not have very good voices. They cannot crow.'

After that, he insisted on being called 'Lord Cockerel' by the other animals.

'Respect, where respect is due!' he called severely. 'What? What? What? Respect me!'

At last, the rest of the farmyard creatures said that they could stand it no longer.

'He needs to be taught a lesson,' they decided. 'We'll kidnap him, and shut him up in the corn shed for a week or two. There's plenty to eat there, so he won't be hungry, and it will show him that ordinary folk can manage quite well without such an outcry.'

'Yes! That's a glor-i-ous idea,' mewed the cat.

Kidnapping Lord Cockerel wasn't so easy as they had thought it was going to be. He was so alert and watchful, stepping proudly

among them and darting his fierce yellow eyes in all directions. Once, Pig lumbered up behind him with a sack, and was just about to drop it over his head when Lord Cockerel turned and saw him.

'What? What? What? What are you going to do?' he cackled.

'Just gathering acorns,' answered Pig hastily. 'Tra-la ... tra-la ... tum tiddly um tum ...' He wandered off.

On another occasion, Cow almost succeeded in pushing him into her milking pail. But she stumbled and kicked it over in her efforts, and Lord Cockerel made a great fuss about the spilled milk. 'A stupid thing to doooo!' he crowed crossly.

They had almost given up hope when Cat thought of a plan.

'It's a very de-vi-ous plan,' she mewed. 'I will pretend I have hurt my tail. I will hide under the sacks in the corn shed and cry for help. When Lord Cockerel comes in to see what has happened, I will run out quickly and shut the door on him, and push the bolt across on the outside with my paw. I can do that,' she explained, 'because I am a member of the CAT family. Cats are clever. Everybody knows that.'

The plan worked splendidly. Cat made a pitiful outcry, mewing that her tail was caught in a trap. Lord Cockerel stalked into the corn shed to advise her, and in half a second she had whisked past him, slammed the door and pushed home the bolt.

He was caught.

It was no use crowing, either. The corn shed was a long way from the farmhouse. No one would hear him.

The aimals were delighted with the success of their trick. The yard was peaceful and friendly; it seemed a different place. The donkey dozed in the meadow ... the swallows nested in the eaves ... the hens made dustbaths for themselves and fluttered and gossiped together.

At last, dusk fell.

'There's just one thing,' Cat reminded them, as she dropped in for a last taste of milk. 'Someone will have to rouse the Farmer in the morning, otherwise he won't get up. Human beings never do. They are not like us. They would sleep all day as well as all night if there were no interruption.'

The aimals nodded their heads and nudged each other.

'Cat is sensible,' they said. 'Let Pig rouse the Farmer in the morning. He has a good, loud grunt. But who will wake Pig?'

'The swallows in the eaves will wake me,' answered Pig. 'They always start the day early. They twitter and flutter like ever so.'

So they all went to bed and slept.

Sure enough, as soon as it was light the swallows began tweeting and fidgeting. Pig opened one eye ... then the other. He yawned. Then, feeling important, he lumbered over to the farmhouse, took up a position beneath the bedroom windows, and grunted:

'SNORK
   SNORK
      SNUMP!'

'George,' whispered Alice. 'That pig's making a dreadful noise. He

37

must have got a stomach-ache. Best take him to the Vet, before it gets any worse!'

George raised himself on his elbow, and listened.

'SNORK
  SNORK
    SNUMP!'

'You're right, Alice. I'll just have a bite of breakfast, and we'll be off. Luckily, the Vet'll be in the village at nine. It's his day. He'll soon put him right. You may be sure of that.'

He lurched out of bed, pulled on his trousers and sweater, and swallowed some hot tea. Then, without more ado, he chivied Pig into the wheelbarrow and wheeled him off...

The other animals watched them go. They felt a little uneasy.

Hours later, the wheelbarrow returned, with a crestfallen Pig.

'What happened, old chap?' asked Donkey sympathetically.

'The Vet said I had over-eaten,' answered Pig crossly. 'I'm to have nothing but warm water and bicarbonate for a week. Such an idea! I shall starve to death. *You* can wake the Farmer next time. I shan't.'

He stumped heavily back to his sty and slammed the door.

'Poor fellow!' mooed Cow. 'Tomorrow morning, I'll go. Leave it to me. The farmer understands my language. I often call to him when it is milking time, to remind him to bring a pail. I'll wake him.'

'You are sure to be more successful, my dear,' agreed Cat. She did not want to go herself, for she was fond of her sleep and had no intention of rising early. 'I *think* what to do, *they* do it,' she purred.

As soon as she heard the swallows moving in the rafters, Cow raised her head, threw back her shoulders and ambled purposefully towards the farmhouse.

Under the window grew a fine hawthorn hedge. Cow took a mouthful or two, for she was partial to hawthorn and found the prickly bits especially delicious. Then:

'MOO!'

Alice was at the bedroom window in a second, peering under the curtain. 'George,' she cried desperately. 'That cow's on the flower bed! She's trampling on the roses! She's eating the hedge! Stop her! Stop her! Get her off!'

'Well! Did you ever hear such a thing?' marvelled George, staring blearily over his wife's shoulder. 'Drat her! We'll empty a load of water over her – that'll make her change her ways!' And without another word, he filled the slop pail and tipped it over the sill.

Sssssssssssplashshshshshshshshs!

Cow stepped back hastily. She disliked water, except for drinking purposes, and some of it had gone in her eye. Hurriedly, she made her way back to the barn, stamping her feet and rubbing up against the straw to warm herself.

'Raining?' questioned Donkey pleasantly. He was half awake.

'It's *not* raining!' snapped Cow. 'I expect I've caught pneuuuuuuuumonia. Moo! I shan't wake him tomorrow morning. That's certain. It's *your* turn.'

Donkey sniffed.

But nobody else volunteered. The animals were beginning to feel uncomfortable. Perhaps they had been rather silly to kidnap Lord Cockerel after all. He *was* good at waking people up. No one could deny that.

'What about Dog?' muttered Donkey hopefully. 'Let Dog do it. A dog is Man's Best Friend.'

But Dog wouldn't.

'Let them sleep,' he growled. 'They like sleeping. Why shouldn't they? They'll get up some time, I dare say ... next week ... or the week after. In time for Christmas. They won't want to miss the puddin', you see. *She*'ll cook it. *He*'ll eat it. They look forward to that. It's what they like, puddin'. Mind you, I prefer a good bone myself, nicely matured, and with a maggot or two. But there's no accounting for tastes.'

'What about Cat?'

'Me?' squeaked Cat. 'The idea! I don't *do* things of that kind. I tell other people how to do them. It's what we call delegation. I know howwww, you see, so I tell them. But my voice is far, far too delicate to emulate an alarm clock.'

She rolled the word emulate round her tongue. It was a long word. Nobody knew what it meant.

'*All* right,' snuffed Donkey. 'I will, then. I'll wake him. But only once.'

Night fell. It was damp and misty. Owls hooted from the elm trees and there wasn't a moon at all – only a pale sort of wish-wash where she might have been.

'It's a pity to disturb a person's rest,' thought Donkey to himself, in his muddled way. 'I'll go and wake the Farmer *now*, before he goes to sleep. Then the job'll be done. That's a brilliant idea, that is. Brains ... that's what's needed. Brains.'

He pushed open the door of the outhouse with his nose and made his way towards the farm. But it wasn't where he thought it should have been. He had forgotten how difficult it is to find anyone, anything, anywhere, at night. He blundered and stumbled ... he scraped his shins against the water trough ... he tripped over Dog's feeding bowl ...

'George,' whispered Alice.

'Ah?'

'I hear burglars.'

'Burglars?'

'In the yard. Listen.'

Bump, bump, bump.

Then, 'EEE OOR!' sounded through the darkness.

'EE OOR! EEEEEEE OR! I might as well make as much row as I can,' muttered Donkey, 'in case I'm in the wrong place.'

He took an enormous breath.

'EEEE OORR!'

'It's that donkey, my dear,' grunted George. 'We'll throw something in his direction – to send him away. Stupid creature. He thinks it's morning.'

A piece of soap hurtled out of the bedroom window.

'Carrots?' questioned Donkey, as he caught it neatly. 'Ugh! Soap!'

Blowing bubbles, spluttering, hiccuping, he galloped across the farmyard and disappeared into the meadow. They could hear his footsteps growing fainter ... fainter ... Then silence.

'He'd better sleep outside in future,' the Farmer decided. 'Maybe he doesn't like being in a shed.'

George and Alice finished undressing, pulled the eiderdown up to their chins, and slept.

Well, all stories have an ending. Before many hours had passed, it was heard that *somebody* had pulled back the bolt on the door of the corn shed. *Who* did it, nobody knew.

'It was the wind, I dare say,' mewed Cat drowsily. 'Or weasels. Ask no questions, you'll be told no lies. Anyway, Lord Cockerel is at large again. We ALL know that. Listen!'

'Cock-a-doodle-doo!' shrilled from corner of the rickyard.

But it did not sound quite so jaunty as before.

'Get up, good people, do!' called a familiar voice. Lord Cockerel fluttered towards them, clearing his throat.

'Been away for a brief holiday,' he explained. 'And – listen will you? I don't want to be called Lord Cockerel any more. Just Cockerel. Or Cocky, for short. See? Cocky!'

He has been known as Cocky for some time, now. And he is *much* more thoughtful than he used to be. When the animals are dozing, he only crows in a whisper. Like this:

'*Cock-a-doodle-doo.*'

The rest of them have really grown quite fond of him.

'We all have our peculiarities,' explained Cat, washing carefully behind her left ear. 'What one can't do another can.'

The animals nodded. They knew *that* was right. Why, who would expect Donkey to lay eggs, or Dog to fill the milk churns?

'Furthermore,' went on Cat, yawning and arching her back, 'nobody tells the truth, the whole truth, and nothing but the truth – *all* day long.

'Who *could* have let Cocky out? I know, mind you. But I shan't say.

'Mew!'

JEAN KENWARD

41

'FRAIDY MOUSE

Once upon a time there were three grey mice, and they lived in a corner of a barn.

Two of the mice weren't afraid of anything, except the brown tabby cat who lived in the farmhouse. Two of the mice said, 'Hi! Look at us. We're tricky and we're quicky and we're fighty and we're bitey. We're not afraid of anything, except the tabby cat.'

But the third little mouse said, 'Don't look at me. I'm afraid of everything. I'm a 'Fraidy Mouse.'

'Fraidy Mouse's brothers said, 'Don't be ridiculous. There's nothing to be frightened of, except the tabby cat.'

'Fraidy Mouse shivered, 'I've never seen a tabby cat. Does Tabby Cat stamp with his feet? Does he growl?'

'Fraidy Mouse's brothers said, 'Don't be absurd. Tabby Cat sits by the door of the barn.

> *He sits on the ground,*
> *He's big and he's round.*
> *He doesn't move a muscle*
> *Till he hears a little rustle.*
> *Then he'll jump. Thump!*
> *And he'll eat you till you're dead.'*

Then 'Fraidy Mouse's brothers said, 'But Tabby Cat's indoors now. So off we go together to be bold, brave mice.'

'Fraidy Mouse was left alone, sitting in the barn. In case he should see something fearsome and frightening, he closed his eyes tightly and fell fast asleep.

While 'Fraidy Mouse was sleeping, the farmer passed the barn. He was carrying a sack full of big brown potatoes. One of the potatoes fell out and rolled about. It rolled to the door of the barn. And there it stayed.

'Fraidy Mouse woke up. He saw that big potato. 'Mercy me! It's Tabby Cat, sitting by the door!

He's sitting on the ground,
And he's big and he's round.
He won't move a muscle
Till he hears a little rustle.
Then he'll jump. Thump!
And he'll eat me till I'm dead.'

'Fraidy Mouse kept so still that all his bones were aching. Then his brothers came back, and they said, 'Hi, 'Fraidy Mouse!'

'Fraidy Mouse whispered, 'Hush! Oh hush! Don't you see the tabby cat sitting by the door?'

'Fraidy Mouse's brothers said, 'Don't be idiotic. That's not a tabby cat. That's a big potato.' And they laughed. 'Fraidy Mouse's brothers rolled around laughing, until they were exhausted and had to go to sleep.

But poor little 'Fraidy Mouse cried himself to sleep.

While the mice were sleeping, the farmer passed the barn. He picked the potato up and carried it away. 'Fraidy Mouse twitched in his sleep – dreaming. He dreamed he was a tricky, quicky little mouse.

As the sun went down, the big brown tabby cat came padding to the barn. And he sat by the door. 'Fraidy Mouse twitched in his sleep again – dreaming. He dreamed he was a fighty, bitey little mouse.

After a while, the mice woke up. The first thing they saw in the twilight was the cat, a big round brown thing sitting by the door. 'Fraidy Mouse's brothers hid away in holes. They stared out with frightened eyes, too terrified to speak.

'Fraidy Mouse thought they were teasing him again, pretending to be frightened of a big brown potato. He wouldn't get caught like *that* again!

He called out, 'Hi there! You silly old potato!' The tabby cat was so surprised he didn't move a muscle. 'Fraidy Mouse called again, 'I'm only small and 'Fraidy. But I'm not afraid of *you*, you silly old potato. And neither are my tricky, quicky, fighty, bitey brothers.'

Tabby Cat said to himself, 'What a mouse! If that's a little 'Fraidy Mouse, the smallest, most afraid mouse, his brothers must be terrible. I shan't come here again.'

Then Tabby Cat stalked away, pretending not to hurry. And 'Fraidy Mouse said, 'Funny! That potato's got a tail!'

'Fraidy Mouse's tricky, quicky, fighty, bitey brothers came creeping from their holes, and they said, 'Oh, 'Fraidy Mouse! How brave you were to talk to the tabby cat like that!'

'Fraidy Mouse thought, 'Tabby Cat! That wasn't a potato. I was talking to a real live tabby cat. Oh my!'

Then his legs gave way, and he fell on his back. And his brothers said, 'He's resting. It's tiring being so brave!'

ANNE WELLINGTON

J. ROODIE

J. Roodie was wild and bad, although he was only nine. Nobody owned him, so he lived in a creek bed with his animals, who had nasty names. His dog was called Grip, which was what it did to passers-by. He had a bad-tempered brumby called Kick, and a raggedy crow called Pincher. Pincher swooped down and stole kids' twenty cents worth of chips when they came out of the fish and chip shop. J. Roodie had trained him to do that.

Nobody ever went for a stroll along the creek, because they knew better. J. Roodie kept a supply of dried cow manure and used it as ammunition, because he didn't have pleasant manners at all. He never had a bath and his fingernails were a disgrace and a shame.

There was a cottage near the creek with a FOR SALE notice, but no one wanted to live near J. Roodie. Everyone muttered, 'Someone should do something about that awful J. Roodie!' but nobody knew what to do and they were too scared to get close enough to do it, anyhow.

J. Roodie painted creek-mud scars across his face, and blacked out his front teeth. He drew biro tattoos over his back and he stuck a metal ring with a piece missing through his nose so that it looked pierced. He swaggered around town and pulled faces at babies in prams and made them bawl, and he filled the kindergarten sandpit with quicksand. Luckily the teacher discovered it before she lost any pupils.

He let Grip scare everyone they met, and he let Kick eat people's prize roses, and he was just as much a nuisance going out of town as he was going in. But nobody came and told him off, because they were all nervous of tough J. Roodie and his wild animals.

One day he was annoyed to see that the FOR SALE notice had been removed from the cottage and someone had moved in. He sent Grip over to scare them away.

Grip bared his fangs and slobbered like a hungry wolf at the little old lady who had just moved in.

'Oh, what a sweet puppy!' said the little old lady whose name was Miss Daisy Thrimble. Grip had never been called 'sweet' before, so he stopped slobbering and wagged his tail. Miss Daisy Thrimble gave him a bath and fluffed up his coat with a hair dryer. 'I'll call you Curly,' she said. 'Here's a nice mat for you, Curly.'

Grip felt self-conscious about going back to J. Roodie with his coat all in little ringlets, and besides, the mat was cosier than a creek bed, so he went to sleep.

J. Roodie waited two days for him and then he sent Pincher to the cottage. Miss Daisy was hanging out washing. 'Caaaaawwrk!' Pincher croaked horribly, flapping his big, raggedy, untidy wings and snapping his beak.

'What a poor little lost bird,' said Miss Daisy. She plucked Pincher out of the sky and carried him inside. She filled a saucer with canary seed and fetched a mirror and a bell. 'I'll call you Pretty Boy,' she said. 'And I'll teach you how to talk.'

Pincher already knew some not very nice words that J. Roodie taught him, but Miss Daisy Thrimble looked so sweet-faced and well behaved that Pincher didn't say them. He tapped the bell with his beak, and looked in the little mirror, and decided that it was very nice to have playthings.

J. Roodie grew tired of waiting for Pincher, and he sent Kick to scare Miss Daisy away. Kick pawed the lawn and carried on like a rodeo and rolled his eyes till the whites showed.

'Oh, what a darling little Shetland pony!' said Miss Daisy. She caught Kick and brushed away the creek mud and plaited his mane into rosettes tied up with red ribbons. 'There's a cart in the shed,' she said. 'You can help me do the shopping. I'll call you Twinkle.'

Kick snorted indignantly, but then he saw his reflection in a kitchen window and was amazed that he could look so dignified. He stopped worrying about his new name when Miss Daisy brought him a handful of oats.

J. Roodie marched over to the cottage and yelled, 'YAAAAH!' at the top of his voice. He jumped up and down and brandished a spear and rattled some coconuts with faces painted on them, which were tied to his belt. They looked just like shrunken heads. 'WHEEEEEE!' yelled J. Roodie. 'GRRRRRRR!'

'What a dear little high-spirited boy!' said Miss Daisy. 'But you certainly need a bath.' She dumped J. Roodie into a tub and when she had finished scrubbing, he was as clean and sweet-smelling as an orange. Miss Daisy dressed him in a blue checked shirt and nice clean pants and brushed his hair. 'There,' she said. 'I shall call you Joe. I'll be proud to take you into town with me in my little cart.'

She sat Joe Roodie next to her, and Kick, called Twinkle now,

trotted smartly into town, and Grip, called Curly now, ran beside and didn't nip anyone they met.

People said, 'Good morning, Miss Daisy. Is that your little nephew?'

'His name is Joe,' Miss Daisy said proudly. 'I think he lived in the creek bed before he came to stay with me.'

'He can't have,' they said. 'J. Roodie lives in the creek bed and he'd never let anyone else live there.'

'J. who?' asked Miss Daisy, because she was rather hard of hearing. 'Do you know anyone called J. something or other, Joe?'

Joe Roodie didn't answer right away. He'd just felt in the pockets of his new pants and found a pocket knife with six blades, and a ball of red twine, and some interesting rusty keys, and eleven marbles.

'We'll buy some apples and make a pie for our supper,' said Miss Daisy. 'Maybe we could invite that J. boy they said lives in the creek. What do you think, Joe?'

Joe Roodie hadn't tasted apple pie for as many years as he hadn't had a bath, and his mouth watered.

'There used to be a kid called J. Roodie in the creek bed,' he said. 'But he doesn't live there any more.'

ROBIN KLEIN

48

THE CHRISTMAS ROAST

Once a man found a goose on the beach. The November storms had been raging several days before. She had probably swum too far out, been caught, and then tossed back to land again by the waves. No one in the area had geese. She was a real white domestic goose.

The man stuck her under his jacket and took her home to his wife. 'Here's our Christmas roast.'

They had never kept an animal and had no coop. The man built a little shed out of posts, boards and roofing board right next to the house wall. The woman put sacks in it and put an old sweater on top of them. In the corner they put a pot with water in it.

'Do you know what geese eat?' she asked.

'No idea,' said the man.

They tried potatoes and bread, but the goose wouldn't touch anything. She didn't want any rice either, and she didn't want the rest of their Sunday cake.

'She's homesick for the other geese,' said the woman.

The goose didn't resist when they carried her into the kitchen. She sat quietly under the table. The man and the woman squatted before her, trying to cheer her up.

'But we aren't geese,' said the man. He sat on a chair and tried to find some band music on the radio. The woman sat beside him, her knitting needles going clickety-clack. It was very cosy. Suddenly the goose ate some rolled oats and a little cake.

'She's settling down, our lovely Christmas roast,' said the man. By next morning the goose was waddling all over the place. She stuck her neck through the open doors, nibbled on the curtains, and made a little spot on the doormat.

The house in which the man and woman lived was a simple one. There was no indoor plumbing, only a pump. When the man pumped a bucket full of water, as he did every morning before going to work, the goose came along, climbed into the

49

bucket and bathed. The water spilled over, and the man had to pump again.

In the garden there was a little wooden house, which was the toilet. When the woman went to it, the goose ran behind her and pressed inside with her. Later she went with the woman to the baker and then to the dairy store.

When the man came home from work on his bicycle that afternoon, the woman and the goose were standing at the garden gate.

'Now she likes potatoes, too,' reported the woman.

'Wonderful,' said the man and stroked the goose on the head. 'Then by Christmas she will be round and fat.'

The shed was never used, for the goose stayed in the warm kitchen every night. She ate and ate. Sometimes the woman set her on the scales, and each time she was heavier.

When the man and the woman sat with the goose in the evening, they both imagined the most marvellous Christmas food.

'Roast goose and red cabbage. They go well together,' said the woman and stroked the goose on her lap.

The man would rather have had sauerkraut than red cabbage,

but for him the most important thing was the dumplings. 'They must be as big as my head and all the same size,' he said.

'And made with raw potatoes,' added his wife.

'No, with cooked ones,' asserted the man. Then they agreed that half the dumplings should be made with raw potatoes and half with cooked ones. When they went to bed, the goose lay at the foot and warmed them.

All at once it was Christmas.

The wife decorated a small tree. The husband biked to the shop and bought everything they would need for the great feast. He also bought a kilo of extra-fine rolled oats.

'Even if it's her last,' he said with a sigh, 'she should at least know that it's Christmas.'

'I've been wondering,' began the woman, 'how, do you think, should we ... I mean ... we still have to ...' But she couldn't get any further.

The man didn't say anything for a while. 'I can't do it,' he said finally.

'I can't either,' said the woman. 'I could, if it were just any old goose. But not this one. No, I can't do it, no matter what.'

The man grabbed the goose and fastened her on to his baggage carrier. Then he rode his bicycle to a neighbour's. In the meantime, the woman cooked red cabbage and made the dumplings, one just as big as the next.

The neighbour lived far away, to be sure, but still not so far that it was a day's journey. Nevertheless, the man did not come home until evening. The goose sat contentedly behind him.

'I never saw our neighbour. We just rode around,' he said ashamedly.

'It doesn't matter,' said the woman cheerfully. 'While you were gone, I thought it over and decided that adding something else to the dinner would just spoil the good taste of the red cabbage and the dumplings.'

The woman was right, and they had a good meal. At their feet the goose feasted on the extra-fine rolled oats. Later all three sat together on the sofa in the living room and enjoyed the candlelight.

The next year, for a change, the woman cooked sauerkraut to go with the dumplings. The year afterwards there were broad

noodles to go with the sauerkraut. They were such good things that nothing else was needed to go with them.

And so time passed. Goose grew very old.

MARGRET RETTICH
Translated by ELIZABETH D. CRAWFORD

KING CROOKED-CHIN

A great King had a daughter who was very beautiful, but so haughty that none of the suitors who came to ask her hand in marriage were good enough for her; she only rejected them, and made game of them.

One day the King held a great feast, to which he asked all her lovers; and they sat in a row according to their rank – Kings, and Princes, and Dukes, and Earls. Then the Princess came in and saw them all, but she had something to say against every one. The first was too fat. 'He's as round as a beerbarrel,' she said. The next was too tall. 'What a maypole!' said she. The next was too short. 'What

52

a dumpling!' said she. The fourth was too pale, and she called him 'White-face'. The fifth was too red, so she called him 'Coxcomb'. The sixth was not straight enough, so she said he was like a green stick that had been laid to dry over a baker's oven. And thus she had some joke to crack about every one; but she laughed more than all at a good King who was there, and whose chin was none of the handsomest. 'Look at him,' she said, 'he has a chin, and so has a thrush!' So the King got the nickname of Crooked-Chin.

But the old King was very angry when he saw that his daughter did nothing but laugh at all his guests and despise all the suitors that had been invited to the feast, and he vowed that she should marry the first beggar that came to the door.

Two days after there came by a travelling musician, who began to sing under the window, and to beg money; and when the King heard him, he said; 'Let him come in.' So they brought in a dirty-looking fellow; and when he had sung before the King and the Princess, he begged a boon. Then the King said:

'You have sung so well, that I will give you my daughter there for your wife.'

The Princess was horrified; but the King said: 'I have sworn to give you to the first beggar, and I will keep my word.'

So all entreaties were of no avail. The priest was sent for, and the marriage took place at once. When this was over, the King said:

'Now get ready to go; you must not stay in my palace any longer, but must travel on with your husband.'

Then the beggar departed, and took her with him, and they soon came to a great wood.

'Pray,' said she, 'whose is this wood?'

'It belongs to King Crooked-Chin,' answered he; 'had you taken him, all had been yours.'

'Ah! poor unhappy woman that I am!' sighed she, 'would that I had married King Crooked-Chin!'

Next they came to some fine meadows. 'Whose are these beautiful green meadows?' said she.

'They belong to King Crooked-Chin; had you taken him, they had all been yours.'

'Ah! poor unhappy woman that I am!' said she, 'would that I had married King Crooked-Chin!'

Then they came to a great city. 'Whose is this noble city?' said she.

'It belongs to King Crooked-Chin; had you taken him, it had all been yours.'

'Ah! poor unfortunate woman that I am!' sighed she, 'why did I not marry King Crooked-Chin?'

'That displeases me very much,' said the musician, 'that you should wish for another husband. Am I not good enough for you?'

At last they came to a small cottage. 'What a paltry place!' said she. 'To whom does that wretched little hole belong?'

Then the musician said: 'That is your house and mine, where we are to live.'

'Where are your servants?' cried she.

'Servants!' said he. 'You must serve yourself for whatever you want. Now make the fire, and put on water and cook my supper, for I am very tired.'

But the Princess did not know in the least how to make a fire or cook, and the beggar was forced to help her. When they had eaten a very poor supper, they went to bed; but the musician called

her up very early in the morning to clean the house. Thus they lived in a miserable way for a few days; and when they had eaten up all their provisions, the man said:

'Wife, we can't go on thus, spending all and gaining nothing. You must learn to weave baskets.'

Then he went out and cut willows, and brought them home, and she began to weave; but they cut her delicate fingers.

'I see this work won't do,' said he; 'try to spin. Perhaps that will suit you better.'

So she sat down and tried to spin; but the tough threads cut her tender fingers till they bled again.

'See, now,' said the musician, 'you are fit for no work at all. What a bad bargain I have made! However, I'll try to set up business in the earthenware line, and you shall stand in the market and sell.'

'Alas!' thought she, 'when I stand in the market, and when any of my father's court pass by and see me there, how they will laugh at me!'

But it was of no use complaining; she must either work or starve.

At first the trade went well, for many people, seeing such a beautiful woman, went to buy her wares out of compliment to her, and many even paid their money and left the dishes into the bargain. They lived on this as long as it lasted, and then her husband bought a fresh lot of ware, and she sat down with it all around her in a corner of the market; but a mad soldier soon came by, and rode his horse among her dishes, and broke them all into a thousand pieces. Then she began to cry, and knew not, in her grief, what to do.

'Ah, what will become of me!' said she. 'What will my husband say?' So she ran home and told him all.

'Who would have thought you would have been so silly,' said he, 'as to put earthenware in the corner of the market, where everybody passes? But let us have no more crying. I see you are not fit for any regular work, so I have been to the King's palace, and asked if they did not want a kitchen-maid, and they have engaged to take you for your food.'

Thus the Princess became a kitchen-maid, and helped the cook to do all the dirty work; but she was allowed to carry home in two

jars, one on each side, some of the food that was left, and on this she and her husband lived.

She had not been there long before she heard that the King's eldest son was passing by, on his way to be married; and she went to one of the doors and looked out, and seeing all the pomp and splendour, she thought with an aching heart of her own fate, and bitterly lamented the pride which had brought her to such poverty. And the servants gave her some of the rich meats, which she put into her jars to take home.

All at once the King's son appeared in golden clothes; and when he saw a beautiful woman at the door, he took her by the hand, and said she should be his partner in the dance; but she refused, and was afraid, for she saw that it was King Crooked-Chin, who had been one of her suitors, and whom she had repulsed with scorn. However, he kept fast hold and led her in, and the covers

57

of the jars fell off, so that the food in it was scattered about. Then everybody laughed and jeered at her when they saw this, and she was so ashamed that she wished herself a thousand miles deep in the earth. She sprang to the door to run away; but on the steps King Crooked-Chin overtook her, and brought her back, and said:

'Fear me not! I am the musician who lived with you in the poor hut; and it was because I loved you that I disguised myself like that. I am also the soldier who overset your crockery. I have done all this only to bring down your pride. Now all is over, and it is time to celebrate our wedding.'

Then the maids of honour came and brought her the richest dresses; and her father and his whole court came, and wished her all happiness on her marriage with King Crooked-Chin.

ANON.

ELIZABETH

'What do you want for Christmas?' asked Kate's mother.

'I want a red ball,' said Kate, 'and a new dress and a book and a doll. I want a doll with golden curls who walks and talks and turns somersaults.'

'Well,' said Kate's mother, 'we shall see what surprises Christmas brings.'

It seemed as though Christmas would never come, but of course Christmas came. Kate opened her presents under the tree. There was a red ball and a new dress and a book and other gifts. And underneath them all, in a long white box, there was a doll. It was a soft cloth doll with warm brown eyes and thick brown plaits like Kate's.

'What does it do?' asked Kate.

'Everything a doll's supposed to do,' her mother said.

Kate picked the doll up from its box. Its arms hung limply at its sides. Its weak legs flopped, and they couldn't hold it up. 'What's its name?' asked Kate.

'She doesn't have a name,' Kate's mother said. 'No one has a name until somebody loves her.'

Kate set the doll back in the box. 'Thank you,' she said to her mother politely. 'It's an ugly doll,' she said to herself inside. 'It's an ugly doll, and I hate it very much.'

There were no more presents under the tree.

Kate's cousin Agnes came for Christmas dinner. Agnes had a new doll whose name was Charlotte Louise. Charlotte Louise

could walk and talk. 'Where is your Christmas doll?' asked Agnes.

Kate showed her the cloth doll lying in the box.

'What does it do?' asked Agnes.

'It doesn't do anything,' Kate replied.

'What is its name?' asked Agnes.

'It doesn't have a name,' said Kate.

'It certainly is an ugly doll,' said Agnes. She set Charlotte Louise down on the floor, and Charlotte Louise turned a somersault.

'I hate you, Agnes,' Kate said, 'and I hate your ugly doll!'

Kate was sent upstairs to bed without any Christmas cake.

The next day was the day after Christmas. Kate's mother asked her to put away her presents. Kate put away her red ball and her new dress and her book and all her other gifts except the doll.

'I don't want this ugly doll,' she said to James the collie. 'You may have it if you like.'

James wagged his tail. He took the cloth doll in his mouth and carried it out to the snowy garden.

By lunchtime James hadn't come home, and Kate was sorry she had given her doll to him. She couldn't eat her sandwich or her cake. 'James will chew up that doll,' she said to herself. 'He'll chew and chew until there's nothing left but stuffing and some rags. He'll bury her somewhere in the snow.'

She put on her coat and mittens and boots and went out into the garden. James was nowhere to be seen. 'I'm sorry,' said Kate inside herself. 'I'm very, very sorry, and I want to find my doll.'

Kate looked all over the garden before she found her. The doll was lying under the cherry tree, half-buried in the snow, but except for being wet and cold, she seemed as good as new. Kate brushed her clean and cradled her in her arms. 'It's all right now, Elizabeth,' she said, 'because I love you after all.'

Elizabeth could do everything.

When Kate was happy, Elizabeth was happy.

When Kate was sad, Elizabeth understood.

When Kate was naughty and had to go upstairs, Elizabeth went with her.

Elizabeth didn't care for baths. 'She doesn't like water,' Kate explained, 'because of being buried in the snow.' Elizabeth sat on the edge of the bath and kept Kate company while she scrubbed.

Elizabeth loved to swing and slide and go round and round on the merry-go-round.

When Kate wanted to be the mother, Elizabeth was the baby.

When Kate wanted to be Cinderella, Elizabeth was a wicked stepsister and the fairy godmother too.

Sometimes Kate forgot about Elizabeth because she was playing with other friends.

Elizabeth waited patiently. When Kate came back, Elizabeth was always glad to see her.

In the spring, Elizabeth and Kate picked violets for Kate's mother's birthday and helped Kate's father fly a kite.

In the summer, everyone went to the seaside. Agnes was there too, but Agnes's doll, Charlotte Louise, was not.

'Where is Charlotte Louise?' Kate asked, holding Elizabeth in her arms.

'Charlotte Louise is broken,' Agnes said, 'We threw her in the dustbin. I shall have a new doll for Christmas.'

Agnes wouldn't go into the water. She was afraid. But Kate went in for a dip. She set Elizabeth on a towel to sleep safely in the sun. When she came out of the water, Elizabeth was gone.

'Help,' cried Kate, 'please, somebody help! Elizabeth is drowning!'

Everyone heard the word 'drowning', but nobody quite heard who. Grown-ups shouted and ran around pointing their fingers towards the sea.

> Then out of nowhere
> Like a streak,
> Galloping, galloping,
> James the collie came.

Out into the sea and back to shore he swam, Elizabeth hanging limply from his mouth.

After an hour in the sun, Elizabeth was as good as new.

Everyone except Agnes said that James was brave and good and a hero.

Kate didn't say that Agnes had thrown Elizabeth into the sea, but inside herself she thought that Agnes had.

In the autumn, Elizabeth helped Kate gather berries in the meadow for jams and jellies and berry pies.

Then Christmas came again. Of course there were presents under the tree. For Kate, there was a new sledge and a new dress and a book and other gifts. For Elizabeth, there was a woollen coat and hat, and two dresses, one of them velvet.

Agnes came for Christmas dinner. Agnes had a new doll whose name was Tina Marie.

'Tina Marie can sing songs,' said Agnes. 'She can blow bubbles too, and crawl along the floor.'

Kate held Elizabeth tightly in her arms. 'Well,' said Kate in a whisper, 'Tina Marie is the ugliest doll I ever saw. She is almost as ugly as you.'

Agnes kicked Kate sharply on the leg and said the most dreadful

things to Elizabeth, who was looking particularly nice in her velvet dress.

Agnes's mother was very cross with Agnes.

Agnes spent the rest of the day in disgrace and wasn't permitted any Christmas cake.

'Merry Christmas, Elizabeth,' said Kate as she tucked her into bed, 'and Happy Birthday too! You are the best and most beautiful doll in the world, and I wouldn't swop you for anyone else.'

LIESEL MOAK SKORPEN

HORRIBLE HARRY

This was the Davidson family's first taste of country life. Mr Carter, who had sold them the small farm and orchard, was leaving the district. As he climbed into his truck he heard Dad call out to him. Dad had noticed an old horse standing in the paddock.

'I thought you had sent all your horses to your new property, Mr Carter,' said Dad.

'All except old Harry,' said Mr Carter. 'I decided to leave him here.'

'I couldn't afford to buy a horse just now,' said Dad, frowning.

'I'm not asking you to buy him; I'm *giving* him to you.' Mr Carter looked at Dad slyly. 'He's lived here so long it would break his heart to leave, so I'd like him to stay here with you.'

Dad thanked him; then, back at the house, told Mum, Peter and Sue about Harry.

'How odd of him to *give* us a horse,' mused Mum. 'He seemed a very *mean* man. I really didn't like him at all. Well, I must have been mistaken.'

'Can we ride him?' Peter asked excitedly.

'I'd better have a good look at him first,' said Dad. 'Remember, you've never ridden before.' After a closer look at Harry, Dad admitted that it would be almost impossible for anyone to fall off his back; he was nearly as wide as he was long. 'Very low-slung too,' muttered Dad.

'What a funny-looking horse,' said Peter, feeling very disappointed.

'He's hardly what I'd call streamlined,' said Dad. 'Built a bit like an aircraft carrier, isn't he?' Harry swung round and gave Dad a very nasty look. He lifted his top lip and showed a row of large, yellow teeth. 'Don't go too near him,' said Dad. 'He looks a bit wild.'

'I think he's a nice old thing,' said Sue. 'Look, he's smiling!'

'I don't think it's a smile,' said Dad. 'I think it's a snarl.' He was beginning to wonder why Mr Carter had been so keen to leave Harry behind.

'Here boy! Here Harry!' said Peter, holding out his hand and walking slowly towards the horse. But for every step he went forward, Harry went back two. When Peter had him backed into a corner of the paddock he put his head down and butted the boy like a goat. Then he galloped off into the orchard where he began shaking branches with his teeth, snapping them and knocking fruit to the ground.

They found that Harry always went to the orchard if something greatly annoyed him. He would gallop in and do as much damage as he could, then stalk out again with a look on his face that seemed to say: 'That will show them!' But if he was only slightly annoyed he would content himself with knocking down the clothes-prop and tearing washing off the line.

Next day he must have been feeling more friendly, because he let Peter climb on his back. Or perhaps he wasn't feeling more friendly – he could have had something else on his mind. He went round and round the paddock at a fast, erratic trot. Every few minutes he would do a sort of shuffle and change step, sending Peter lurching from one side of his broad back to the other. He made several attempts to bite Peter on the ankle and tried to scrape him off against the fence. When this failed, he headed towards a clump of blackberry bushes and Peter was scratched and sore by the time he had struggled out of it. He climbed on to Harry's back again, but this time Harry didn't fool around. He galloped straight to the dam, propped at the edge, and threw Peter over his head and into the muddy water. Wading out, a very muddy Peter decided never to try riding Harry again – and that, of course, was what Harry wanted.

On Monday the children started at their new school. Mum finished the unpacking, and Dad spent a busy morning in the orchard.

'I'll run the truck up to the front gate,' he told Mum at lunch time. 'The baker was to have left the bread in the mail box and the post should be here too. I'm expecting an important letter.'

When he reached the front gate, which was nearly a kilometre from the house, Harry was standing there with his head resting on the top rung. The mail box was empty.

'No bread and no mail. That's strange,' thought Dad. 'I'll ring the bakery and the post office from the house.'

'We can't deliver the bread unless you lock up Horrible,' said the baker firmly.

'Horrible?' asked Dad.

'Yes, Horrible the horse,' said the baker.

'The horse's name is Harry,' said Dad, not seeing what that had to do with bread deliveries.

'That's right,' said the baker. 'Horrible Harry. He bites anyone who goes near your front gate. I've had three men bitten by Harry and they won't deliver to your place unless he's locked up.'

The postmaster said the same thing. So, too, did the man who delivered fertilizer, and the TV repair-man, and even the doctor, as Dad discovered later.

'Lock him up! That's more easily said than done,' said Dad bitterly after he had wasted half an hour trying to coax Harry into the storage shed. 'All right then!' he spluttered, 'I'll go into town and pick up the bread and the mail myself!' He drove off in an angry cloud of dust, but looked back just in time to see Harry strolling into the storage shed all by himself, for an afternoon rest.

Returning with the bread and mail, Dad stopped the truck and climbed out to open the gate. Harry came galloping up and, as Dad reached for the latch, sank his teeth into Dad's hand.

'Ouch!' shouted Dad, jumping back. Harry lifted his top lip and leered. Each time Dad put his hand out, Harry snapped. Several minutes later Mr Timms from the next farm drove by. He pulled up when he saw Dad's plight.

'Old Horrible won't let you in unless you give him some carrots,' he explained. 'You'll always have to bribe him with carrots before he'll let you through the gate. Didn't Carter tell you about Harry before he left?'

'Carter didn't tell me *anything* about Harry,' Dad muttered darkly. He had to drive ten kilometres back into town to buy some carrots just to get through his own front gate.

'I'll sell him tomorrow,' he told Mum.

But the Stock Agent just laughed at him. 'Sell old Horrible? No one would buy him. You couldn't *give* him away around here!'

Peter *did* try to give him away at school, but everyone said they'd rather own a man-eating tiger than Harry. So the Davidsons just had to learn to live with him. They always made sure they had a carrot before going through the front gate, and they tried not to annoy him very much, especially on washing days.

As the fruit ripened and was almost ready for picking, the district was worried by a spate of robberies. Each night one or other of the farms would be robbed. A truck would be backed through the fence, the trees stripped of their fruit, and by morning only the bare trees were to be seen; the fruit was already on its way to the markets. Watch-dogs were doped and police patrols eluded.

'I hope they don't come here,' said Dad, looking worried. 'I can't afford to lose the crop in our first season.'

A few nights later they were awakened by weird snortings and wild shrieks. Dad raced out of the house and down to the bottom of the orchard. A man was half-way up one of the trees and Harry had his ankle firmly between his teeth, trying to haul him down.

A second man was trying to help the first, but every time he came close, Harry lashed out with his hind legs. Seeing Dad, he lifted his head and gave a fearsome neigh. The man in the tree, his ankle freed, jumped clear and the two men raced for their truck. Harry gave chase. From the way the men yelled, he must have managed a couple of good nips on the way. They scrambled into their truck and roared off with Harry tearing after them. He was neighing like a diesel train's horn.

'Well,' said Dad next morning as he repaired the fence the truck had smashed down, 'I don't think we'll have to worry about them coming back; not while we have Harry here.'

'I bet no one has *ever* heard of a horse like Harry before,' said Sue.

'I bet there's never *been* a *watch*-horse before,' said Peter, and they all laughed.

DIANA PETERSEN

THE PRACTICAL PRINCESS

Princess Bedelia was as lovely as the moon shining upon a lake full of waterlilies. She was as graceful as a cat leaping. And she was also extremely practical.

When she was born, three fairies had come to her cradle to give her gifts, as was usual in that country. The first fairy had given her beauty. The second had given her grace. But the third, who was a wise old creature, had said, 'I give her common sense.'

'I don't think much of that gift,' said King Ludwig, raising his eyebrows. 'What good is common sense to a Princess? All she needs is charm.'

Nevertheless, when Bedelia was eighteen years old, something happened which made the King change his mind.

A dragon moved into the neighbourhood. He settled in a dark cave on top of a mountain, and the first thing he did was to send a message to the King. 'I must have a Princess to devour,' the message said, 'or I shall breathe out my fiery breath and destroy the kingdom.'

Sadly, King Ludwig called together his counsellors and read them the message. 'Perhaps,' said the Prime Minister, 'we had better advertise for a knight to slay the dragon? That is what is generally done in these cases.'

'I'm afraid we haven't time,' answered the king. 'The dragon has only given us until tomorrow morning. There is no help for it. We shall have to send him the Princess.' Princess Bedelia had come to the meeting because, as she said, she liked to mind her own business and this was certainly her business.

'Rubbish!' she said. 'Dragons can't tell the difference between Princesses and anyone else. Use your common sense. He's just asking for me because he's a snob.'

'That may be so,' said her father, 'but if we don't send you along, he'll destroy the kingdom.'

'Right!' said Bedelia. 'I see I'll have to deal with this myself.' She left the council chamber. She got the largest and gaudiest of her state robes and stuffed it with straw, and tied it together with string. Into the centre of the bundle she packed about fifty kilos of gunpowder. She got two strong young men to carry it up the mountain for her. She stood in front of the dragon's cave, and called, 'Come out! Here's the Princess!'

The dragon came blinking and peering out of the darkness. Seeing the bright robe covered with gold and silver embroidery, and hearing Bedelia's voice, he opened his mouth wide.

At Bedelia's signal, the two young men swung the robe and gave it a good heave, right down the dragon's throat. Bedelia threw herself flat on the ground, and the two young men ran.

As the gunpowder met the flames inside the dragon, there was a tremendous explosion.

Bedelia got up, dusting herself off. 'Dragons,' she said, 'are not very bright.'

She left the two young men sweeping up the pieces, and she went back to the castle to have her geography lesson.

The lesson that morning was local geography. 'Our kingdom, Arapathia, is bounded on the north by Istven,' said the teacher. 'Lord Garp, the ruler of Istven, is old, crafty, rich and greedy.' At that very moment, Lord Garp of Istven was arriving at the castle. Word of Bedelia's destruction of the dragon had reached him. 'That girl,' said he, 'is just the wife for me.' And he had come with a hundred finely-dressed courtiers and many presents to ask King Ludwig for her hand.

The king sent for Bedelia. 'My dear,' he said, clearing his throat nervously, 'just see who is here.'

'I see. It's Lord Garp,' said Bedelia. She turned to go.

'He wants to marry you,' said the king.

Bedelia looked at Lord Garp. His face was like an old napkin, crumpled and wrinkled. It was covered with warts, as if someone had left crumbs on the napkin. He had only two teeth. Six long hairs grew from his chin, and none on his head. She felt like screaming.

However, she said, 'I'm very flattered. Thank you, Lord Garp.

70

Just let me talk to my father in private for a minute.' When they had retired to a small room behind the throne, Bedelia said to the king, 'What will Lord Garp do if I refuse to marry him?'

'He is rich, greedy and crafty,' said the king unhappily. 'He is also used to having his own way in everything. He will be insulted. He will probably declare war on us, and then there will be trouble.'

She returned to the throne room. Smiling sweetly at Lord Garp, she said, 'My lord, as you know, it is customary for a princess to set tasks for anyone who wishes to marry her. Surely you wouldn't like me to break the custom. And you are bold and powerful enough, I know, to perform any task.'

'That is true,' said Lord Garp smugly, stroking the six hairs on his chin. 'Name your task.'

'Bring me,' said Bedelia, 'a branch from the Jewel Tree of Paxis.'

Lord Garp bowed, and off he went. 'I think,' said Bedelia to her father, 'that we have seen the last of him. For Paxis is fifteen hundred kilometres away, and the Jewel Tree is guarded by lions, serpents and wolves.'

But in two weeks, Lord Garp was back. With him he bore a chest, and from the chest he took a wonderful twig. Its bark was of rough gold. The leaves that grew from it were of fine silver. The twig was covered with blossoms, and each blossom had petals of mother-of-pearl and centres of sapphires, the colour of the evening sky.

Bedelia's heart sank as she took the twig. But then she said to herself, 'Use your common sense, my girl! Lord Garp never travelled three thousand kilometres in two weeks, nor is he the man to fight his way through lions, serpents, and wolves.'

She looked carefully at the branch. Then she said, 'My lord, you know that the Jewel Tree of Paxis is a living tree, although it is all made of jewels.'

'Why, of course,' said Lord Garp. 'Everyone knows that.'

'Well,' said Bedelia, 'then why is it that these blossoms have no scent?'

Lord Garp turned red.

'I think,' Bedelia went on, 'that this branch was made by the jewellers of Istven, who are the best in the world. Not very nice of you, my lord. Some people might even call it cheating.'

Lord Garp shrugged. He was too old and rich to feel ashamed. But like many men used to having their own way, the more Bedelia refused him, the more he was determined to have her.

'Never mind all that,' he said. 'Set me another task. This time, I swear I will perform it.'

Bedelia sighed. 'Very well. Then bring me a cloak made from the skins of the salamanders who live in the Volcano of Scoria.'

Lord Garp bowed, and off he went. 'The Volcano of Scoria,' said Bedelia to her father, 'is covered with red-hot lava. It burns steadily with great flames, and pours out poisonous smoke so that no one can come within a metre of it.'

'You have certainly profited by your geography lessons,' said the King with admiration.

Nevertheless, in a week, Lord Garp was back. This time, he carried a cloak that shone and rippled like all the colours of fire. It was made of scaly skins, stitched together with golden wire as fine as a hair; and each scale was red and orange and blue, like a tiny flame.

Bedelia took the splendid cloak. She said to herself, 'Use your head, miss! Lord Garp never climbed the red-hot slopes of the Volcano of Scoria.'

A fire was burning in the fireplace of the throne room. Bedelia hurled the cloak into it. The skins blazed up in a flash, blackened, and fell to ashes.

Lord Garp's mouth fell open. Before he could speak, Bedelia said, 'That cloak was a fake, my lord. The skins of salamanders who can live in the Volcano of Scoria wouldn't burn in a little fire like that one.'

Lord Garp turned pale with anger. He hopped up and down, unable at first to do anything but splutter.

'Ub – ub – ub!' he cried. Then, controlling himself, he said, 'So be it. If I can't have you, no one shall!'

He pointed a long, skinny finger at her. On the finger was a magic ring. At once, a great wind arose. It blew through the throne room. It sent King Ludwig flying one way and his guards the other. It picked up Bedelia and whisked her off through the air. When

73

she could catch her breath and look about her, she found herself in a room at the top of a tower.

Bedelia peered out of the window. About the tower stretched an empty, barren plain. As she watched, a speck appeared in the distance. A plume of dust rose behind it. It drew nearer and became Lord Garp on horseback.

He rode to the tower and looked up at Bedelia. 'Aha!' he croaked. 'So you are safe and snug, are you? And will you marry me now?'

'Never,' said Bedelia, firmly.

'Then stay there until never comes,' snarled Lord Garp.

Away he rode.

For the next two days, Bedelia felt very sorry for herself. She sat wistfully by the window, looking out at the empty plain. When she was hungry, food appeared on the table. When she was tired, she lay down on the narrow cot and slept. Each day, Lord Garp rode by and asked if she had changed her mind, and each day she refused him. Her only hope was that, as so often happens in old tales, a prince might come riding by who would rescue her.

But on the third day, she gave herself a shake.

'Now then, pull yourself together,' she said sternly. 'If you sit waiting for a prince to rescue you, you may sit here for ever. Be practical! If there's any rescuing to be done, you're going to have to do it yourself.'

She jumped up. There was something she had not yet done, and now she did it. She tried the door.

It opened.

Outside were three other doors. But there was no sign of a staircase, or any way down from the top of the tower.

She opened two of the doors and found that they led into cells just like hers, but empty.

Behind the fourth door, however, lay what appeared to be a haystack.

From beneath it came the sound of snores. And between snores, a voice said, 'Sixteen million and twelve ... *snore* ... sixteen million and thirteen ... *snore* ... sixteen million and fourteen ...'

Cautiously, she went closer. Then she saw that what she had taken for a haystack was in fact an immense pile of blond hair. Parting it, she found a young man, sound asleep.

74

As she stared, he opened his eyes. He blinked at her. 'Who – ?' he said. Then he said, 'Sixteen million and fifteen,' closed his eyes, and fell asleep again.

Bedelia took him by the shoulder and shook him hard. He awoke, yawning, and tried to sit up. But the mass of hair made this difficult.

'What on earth is the matter with you?' Bedelia asked. 'Who are you?'

'I am Prince Perian,' he replied, 'the rightful ruler of – oh dear! here I go again. Sixteen million and ...' His eyes began to close.

Bedelia shook him again. He made a violent effort and managed to wake up enough to continue, '– of Istven. But Lord Garp has put me under a spell. I have to count sheep jumping over a fence, and this puts me to slee – ee – ee –.'

He began to snore lightly.

'Dear me,' said Bedelia. 'I must do something.'

She thought hard. Then she pinched Perian's ear, and this woke him with a start. 'Listen,' she said. 'It's quite simple. It's all in your mind, you see. You are imagining the sheep jumping over the fence – no! don't go to sleep again!

'This is what you must do. Imagine them jumping backwards. As you do, *count* them backwards, and when you get to *one* you'll be wide awake.'

The prince's eyes snapped open. 'Marvellous!' he said. 'Will it work?'

'It's bound to,' said Bedelia. 'For if the sheep going one way will put you to sleep, their going back again will wake you up.'

Hastily, the prince began to count, 'Sixteen million and fourteen, sixteen million and thirteen, sixteen million and twelve ...'

'Oh, my goodness,' cried Bedelia, 'count by hundreds, or you'll never get there.'

He began to gabble as fast as he could, and with each moment that passed, his eyes sparkled more brightly, his face grew livelier, and he seemed a little stronger, until at last he shouted, 'Five, four, three, two, ONE!' and awoke completely.

He struggled to his feet, with a little help from Bedelia.

'Heavens!' he said. 'Look how my hair and beard have grown.

I've been here for years. Thank you, my dear. Who are you, and what are you doing here?'

Bedelia quickly explained.

Perian shook his head. 'One more crime of Lord Garp's,' he said. 'We must escape and see that he is punished.'

'Easier said than done,' Bedelia replied. 'There are no stairs in this tower, as far as I can tell, and the outside wall is much too smooth to climb.'

Perian frowned. 'This will take some thought,' he said. 'What we need is a long rope.'

'Use your common sense,' said Bedelia. 'We haven't any rope.'

Then her face brightened, and she clapped her hands. 'But we have your beard,' she laughed.

Perian understood at once, and chuckled. 'I'm sure it will reach almost to the ground,' he said. 'But we haven't any scissors to cut it off with.'

'That is so,' said Bedelia. 'Hang it out of the window and let me climb down. I'll search the tower and perhaps I can find a ladder, or a hidden staircase. If all else fails, I can go for help.'

She and the Prince gathered up great armfuls of the beard and staggered into Bedelia's room, which had the largest window. The prince's long hair trailed behind and nearly tripped him.

He threw the beard out of the window, and sure enough the end of it came to within a metre of the ground.

Perian braced himself, holding the beard with both hands to ease the pull on his chin. Bedelia climbed out of the window and slid down the beard. She dropped to the ground and sat for a moment, breathless.

And as she sat there, out of the wilderness came the drumming of hoofs, a cloud of dust, and then Lord Garp on his swift horse.

With one glance, he saw what was happening. He shook his fist up at Prince Perian.

'Meddlesome fool!' he shouted. 'I'll teach you to interfere.'

He leaped from the horse and grabbed the beard. He gave it a tremendous yank. Head first came Perian, out of the window. Down he fell. and, with a thump, he landed right on top of old Lord Garp.

This saved Perian, who was not hurt at all. But it was the end of Lord Garp.

Perian and Bedelia rode back to Istven on Lord Garp's horse.

In the great city, the Prince was greeted with cheers of joy – once everyone had recognized him after so many years and under so much hair.

And of course, since Bedelia had rescued him from captivity, she married him. First, however, she made him get a haircut and a shave so that she could see what he really looked like.

For she was always practical.

JAY WILLIAMS

THE WHITE DOVE

A long time ago, in a country by the sea, there lived a King and Queen who had two sons. And those two sons were reckless lads. One stormy day they put to sea in a little boat to go fishing. The wind howled, and they laughed. The waves dashed over the boat, and still they laughed. But when they were a long way from land, the wind tore their sail to ribbons, and the waves washed their oars overboard; and there they were, tossing about with the waves drenching them, while they clung to their seats to keep from being pitched out of the boat.

'Brother,' said one Prince, 'shall we ever reach home again?'

'No, brother,' said the other. 'It seems we shall not.'

Then they looked through the spray and saw the strangest vessel in the world come speeding towards them over the rolling billows. It was a kneading-trough, and in it sat an old witch, beating the waves with two long wooden ladles.

'Hey, my lads!' she yelled. 'What will you give me to send you safely home?'

'Anything we have!' shouted the Princes.

'Then give me your brother,' yelled the witch.

'We have no brother,' shouted the Princes.

'Aye, but you will have,' yelled the witch.

'Even so,' shouted the eldest Prince, 'should our mother bear another son, he will not belong to us.'

'So we can't give him away!' shouted the other Prince.

'Then you can rot in the salt sea, both of you!' yelled the witch. 'But I think your mother would rather keep the two sons she has than the one she hasn't yet got.' And she rowed off in her kneading-trough.

If the storm had been fierce before, it was now furious. The Princes' little boat was flung up high on the waves one moment, and the next sucked deep down, with the waves towering over it. It pitched and rolled and wallowed and filled with water.

'Brother,' said one Prince, 'we are going to drown.'

'Ah, how our mother will grieve!' said the other Prince.

'Brother,' said the first Prince, 'the old witch was right. Our mother would rather keep *us* than a son she may never have.'

So they shouted after the witch, and she turned her trough and came rowing back to them.

'Have you changed your minds?' she yelled.

'Yes,' shouted the Princes. 'If you will save us from drowning, we promise you the brother we may never have.'

Immediately the wind ceased howling and the sea grew flat. A current caught the boat and drove it swiftly over the calm water. The current brought the boat ashore just under the King's castle. The Princes sprang out, and ran into the castle. The Queen, who had been watching the storm from a window, flung her arms round them.

'Oh my sons!' cried the Queen. 'If you had been drowned I could not have lived!'

And one Prince whispered to the other, 'We did right to promise.'

But they said nothing to their mother about what they had promised, either then, or a year later, when a brother was born to them. The new little Prince was a beautiful child; and because he was so much younger than his brothers, the Queen did her best to spoil him. But it seemed he was unspoilable. He loved his brothers, and they loved him: and still they said nothing about their promise to give him to the witch. For some time, indeed, they lived in dread lest the witch should come and claim him; but, as the years passed, and the little Prince grew up, and still the witch did not come, the two elder Princes almost succeeded in forgetting the promise they had made.

Now the youngest Prince was studious; and often, long after the rest of the household had gone to their beds, he would sit in a little room downstairs, reading and thinking. One night, as he so sat, the wind began to howl and the sea to roar, the stars disappeared behind mountainous black clouds, and the rain came down in torrents. The Prince lifted his head, listened for a moment, and went on reading. Then came three loud knocks on the door; and before the Prince could open it, in darted the witch, with her kneading-trough on her back.

'Come with me!' she said.

The Prince said, 'Why should I go with you?'

'Because you belong to me,' said the witch. And she told him all about that day on which his brothers came near to drowning, and how she had saved their lives, and what they had promised.

The young Prince closed his book and stood up. 'Since you saved my brothers' lives and they gave you their promise, I am ready to go with you,' he said

He followed the witch out of the castle and down to the sea. The witch launched her kneading-trough. They both got into it, and away they went, pitching and tossing over the raging waves, till they came to the witch's home.

'Now you are my servant ' said the witch, 'and everything I tell you to do, you must do. If you cannot do what I tell you to do, you are of no use to me. And when things are of no use to me, I throw them into the sea.'

'I will do my best,' said the young Prince.

The witch then took him to a barn which was piled high with feathers of different colours and sizes. 'Arrange these feathers in their heaps,' she said, 'and let the feathers in each heap be of the same colour and the same size. I am going out now, and when I come back in the evening I shall expect the task to be finished.'

'I will do my best,' said the Prince again.

Ho, ho! But will your best be good enough?' said she.

'That I cannot tell,' said he.

The witch went away then, and the Prince began his task. He worked very hard all day, and towards evening he had all the feathers except one goose quill arranged in their heaps – size to size and colour to colour. He was just going to place the goose quill on top of a heap of big white feathers, when there came a whirlwind that blew the feathers all about the barn. And when the whirlwind had passed and the feathers had settled, they were in worse confusion than they had been at first.

The Prince set to work again; but there was now only an hour left before the time the witch would return. 'I cannot possibly finish by then!' he said aloud. But still he went on with his task.

Then he heard a tapping at the window, and a little voice said:

Coo, coo, coo, please let me in,
If we work together, we'll always win.

It was a white dove, who was perched outside the glass, and was tapping on it with her beak.

The Prince opened the window, and the dove flew in. She set to work with her beak, he set to work with his hands; he worked swiftly, but she worked a hundred times more swiftly. By the time the hour was passed, all the feathers were neatly arranged in their heaps. The dove flew out of the window, and the witch came in at the door.

'So,' said she, 'I see Princes have neat fingers!'

'I have done my best,' said the Prince.

'And tomorrow you must do better,' said she. And she gave him some supper and sent him to bed.

In the morning she took him outside and showed him a great pile of firewood. 'Split this into small pieces for me,' she said. 'That is easy work, and will soon be done. But you must have it all ready by the time I come home.'

'I will do my best,' said the young Prince.

'If your best is not good enough, the sea is waiting,' said the witch. And off she went.

The Prince set to work with a will; he chipped and chopped till the sweat ran off him. But the more wood he chopped up, the more there seemed to be left unchopped. Yes, there was no doubt about it – the pile of unchopped firewood was growing and growing. He flung down his axe in despair. What could he do?

Then the white dove came flying, settled on the pile of wood, and said:

> *Coo, coo, coo, take the axe by the head,*
> *And chop with the handle end instead.*

The Prince took the axe by the head and began chopping with the handle; and the firewood flew into small pieces of its own accord. The Prince chopped, the dove took the little pieces in her beak and arranged them in a tidy pile. In no time at all, it seemed, the task was finished.

Then the dove flew up on to the prince's shoulder. And he stroked its soft feathers. 'How can I ever thank you?' he said. And he kissed its little red beak.

Immediately the dove vanished; and there, at the Prince's side, stood a beautiful maiden.

'How can I ever thank *you*,' said the maiden, 'for the kiss that has disenchanted me?'

She told him that she was a Princess, whom the witch had stolen and turned into a white dove.

'But the power of a grateful kiss is stronger than all the witch's enchantments,' said the maiden. 'And perhaps together we may find a way to escape her. That is, if you like me well enough?'

'I love you!' said the Prince. And truly, so he did.

'Then listen carefully to what I am going to tell you,' said the Princess. 'When the witch comes home ask her to grant you a wish, as a reward for having accomplished the tasks she has set you. If she agrees, ask her to give you the Princess who is flying about in the shape of a white dove. She will not want to do so; she will try to deceive you; but take this red silk thread and tie it round my little finger. Then you will recognize me, whatever shape she may turn me into.'

So the Prince tied the red silk thread round the Princess's little finger, and she turned into a dove again, and flew away. The Prince sat down by the pile of split firewood to wait until the witch came home. And very soon he saw her coming, with her kneading-trough on her back.

'Well, well, well!' said she. 'I see you are a clever fellow! I think I shall be pleased with you yet!'

'If you are pleased with me,' said the Prince, 'perhaps you will be willing to grant me a little pleasure also, and give me something I have taken a fancy to?'

'Well, well, that's only reasonable,' said the witch, who was in a very good temper. 'Tell me what it is you wish for, and if it is any little thing that is in my power to give you, I promise I will do so.'

'There is a Princess here, who flies about in the shape of a white dove,' said the Prince. 'It is that Princess I want.'

The witch screeched with laughter. 'What nonsense are you talking? As if Princesses ever flew around in the shape of white doves!'

'Nevertheless, I ask for that Princess,' said the Prince.

'Well, well, if you *will* have a Princess,' said the witch, 'you must take the only sort I have.' And she went away round the back of the house, and came again dragging by one long ear a shaggy little grey ass. 'Will you have this?' she said. 'You can't get any other kind of Princess here.'

The Prince looked at the little ass, and saw a thin thread of red silk round one of its hoofs. 'Yes, I will have it,' he said.

'It is too small for you to ride, and too old to draw a cart,' said the witch. 'Why should you have it? It is no use to you at all!' And she dragged the little ass away, and came back with a tottering, trembling old hag of a woman who was blind in one eye, and hadn't a tooth in her head.

'Here's a pretty Princess for you!' said the witch. 'What do you say, will you have her? She was born a Princess, and she's the only one I've got.'

'Yes, I will have her,' said the Prince, for he saw that the old hag had a thin thread of red silk bound about her little finger.

He took the old hag by the hand. Behold – there stood the Princess! The witch flew into such a terrible rage that she danced about and screamed and smashed everything within her reach, so that the splinters flew about the heads of the Prince and Princess. But she had promised the Prince that he should have his wish, and she had to keep her word. She said to herself, 'Yes, they shall be married. But when they *are* married, oh ho! let them look out!'

So the day of the wedding was fixed, and the Princess said to the Prince, 'At the wedding feast you may eat what you please, but you must not drink anything at all; for the witch will put a spell on both the water and the wine, and if you drink you will forget me.'

'How could I ever forget you?' said the Prince.

'Nevertheless, do not drink,' said the Princess.

A whole troop of witches came to the wedding feast. It was a hideous affair, and all the food was so highly seasoned that the Prince's throat was dry and burning. At last he could bear his thirst no longer, and he stretched out his hand for a cup of wine. But the Princess was keeping watch over him; she gave the Prince's arm a push with her elbow: all the wine was spilled over the tablecloth, and the cup rolled off the table and fell on the floor.

When the witch saw that she had been again foiled by the Princess, she flew once more into a terrible rage. She leaped up and laid about her among the plates and dishes, till the splinters flew about the room. The other witches howled with laughter, and joined in the fun, smashing everything they could lay hands on. But when the clamour was at its height, the Princess took the Prince by the hand, and whispered, 'Come!'

They ran up to the bridal chamber which had been got ready for them. And the Princess said, 'The witch had to keep her promise, and we are married. But it was sore against her will, and now she will seek to destroy us. We must escape while we may.'

From having lived so long with the witch, the Princess had learned some magic. Now she took two pieces of wood, spoke some whispered words to them, and laid them side by side in the bed.

'These will answer for us if the witch calls,' she said. 'Now take the flower pot from the ledge, and the bottle of water from the table, and help me down out of the window.'

The Prince picked up the flower pot and the water bottle, helped the Princess down out of the window, and scrambled out after her.

Then off they ran, hand in hand, through the dark night.

The nearest way to reach the Prince's home was across the sea. But they had no boat, so they had to run round the shore of a great bay. All night they were running. Meanwhile, at midnight, the witch went to the door of the bridal chamber, and called, 'Are you sleeping yet?'

And the two pieces of wood answered from the bed, 'No, we are waking.'

The witch went away. Before dawn she came again to the door of the bridal chamber, and called, 'Are you sleeping yet?'

And the two pieces of wood answered from the bed, 'We are waking still. But leave us now to sleep.'

The witch chuckled. 'Sleep soundly,' she muttered. 'You will not wake again in a hurry! For dawn brings a new day. Your wedding night will then be over. And what did I promise you? No more than that!'

She went to her window and watched impatiently for the rising of the new day. As soon as the rim of the sun appeared above the sea, she rushed to the bridal chamber again. But this time she did not stand at the door. She flung the door open, and bounded into the room.

'I have you now!' she screamed.

But what did she see? No Prince, no Princess: only two blocks of wood lying side by side in the bed.

'Ah, ah, ah!' she shrieked. She seized upon the blocks of wood and flung them to the floor so violently that they flew into hundreds of pieces. Then she rushed off after the runaways.

The Prince and Princess had run on through the night. They were still running now along the shore of the bay, with the first beams of the sun on their faces.

Said the Princess, 'Look round. Do you see anything behind us?'
Said the Prince, 'Yes, I see a dark cloud, far away.'
Said the Princess, 'Throw the flower pot over your head.'
The Prince threw the flower pot over his head, and a huge range

of hills rose up behind them. The witch came to the hills; she tried to climb them. But they were smooth and slippery as glass; every time she clambered up a little way, she slid down again. There was nothing for it but to run round the whole range, and that took her a very long time.

The Prince and Princess were still running along the shore of the bay. By and by the Princess said again, 'Look round. Do you see anything behind us?'

'Yes,' said the Prince, 'the big black cloud is there again.'

Said the Princess, 'Throw the bottle of water over your head.'

The Prince threw the bottle of water over his head, and a huge, turbulent lake spread out behind them. The witch came to the lake. It was so huge and so rough that she had to go all the way home again to fetch her kneading-trough before she could cross it.

By the time the witch had crossed the lake and was pelting on again, the Prince and Princess had rounded the bay and reached the castle which was the Prince's home. They climbed over the wall of the keep, and were just about to clamber into the castle through an open window, when the witch caught up with them.

'Ah! Ah! Ah! I have you now!' she screamed.

But the Princess turned and blew upon the witch. A great flock of white doves flew out of the Princess's mouth. They fluttered and flapped about the witch; she was completely hidden by their beating wings. And when the

doves rose into the air and flew away, there was no witch. There was only a great grey stone standing outside the window.

The Prince led his Princess into his father's castle. 'I have come back to you,' he said to the King and Queen. 'And I have brought my bride with me.'

How they all rejoiced! The Prince's two elder brothers came and knelt at his feet and begged his forgiveness. 'You shall inherit the kingdom,' they said, 'and we will be for ever your faithful subjects.' And, in the course of time, when the old King died, that was what happened.

In the meantime, and ever afterwards, they lived in happiness.

RUTH MANNING-SANDERS

BABA YAGA*
AND THE LITTLE GIRL WITH
THE KIND HEART

Once upon a time there was a widowed old man who lived alone in a hut with his little daughter. Very merry they were together, and they used to smile at each other over a table just piled with bread and jam. Everything went well, until the old man took it into his head to marry again.

Yes, the old man became foolish in the years of his old age, and he took another wife. And so the poor little girl had a stepmother. And after that everything changed. There was no more bread and jam on the table, and no more playing bo-peep, first this side of the samovar and then that, as she sat with her father at tea. It was worse than that, for she never did sit at tea. The stepmother said that everything that went wrong was the little girl's fault.

*Baba Yaga is the traditional witch of Russian folklore.

And the old man believed his new wife, and so there were no more kind words for his little daughter. Day after day the stepmother used to say that the little girl was too naughty to sit at table. And then she would throw her a crust, and tell her to get out of the hut, and go and eat it somewhere else.

And the poor little girl used to go away by herself into the shed in the yard, and wet the dry crust with her tears, and eat it all alone. Ah me! she often wept for the old days, and she often wept at the thought of the days that were to come.

Mostly she wept because she was all alone, until one day she found a little friend in the shed. She was hunched up in a corner of the shed, eating her crust and crying bitterly, when she heard a little noise. It was like this: scratch, scratch. It was just that, a little grey mouse who lived in a hole.

Out he came, his little pointed nose and his long whiskers, his little round ears and his bright eyes. Out came his little humpy body and his long tail. And then he sat up on his hind-legs, and curled his tail twice round himself and looked at the little girl.

The little girl, who had a kind heart, forgot all her sorrows, and took a scrap of her crust and threw it to the little mouse. The mouseykin nibbled and nibbled, and there, it was gone, and he was looking for another. She gave him another bit, and presently that was gone, and another and another, until there was no crust left for the little girl. Well, she didn't mind that. You see, she was so happy seeing the little mouse nibbling and nibbling.

When the crust was done the mouseykin looks up at her with his little bright eyes, and 'Thank you,' he says, in a little squeaky voice. 'Thank you,' he says; 'you are a kind little girl, and I am only a mouse, and I've eaten all your crust. But there is one thing I can do for you, and that is to tell you to take care. The old woman in the hut (and that was the cruel stepmother) is own sister to Baba Yaga, the bony-legged, the witch. So if ever she sends you on a message to your aunt, you come and tell me. For Baba Yaga would eat you soon enough with her iron teeth if you did not know what to do.'

'Oh, thank you,' said the little girl; and just then she heard the stepmother calling to her to come in and clean up the tea things, and tidy the house, and brush out the floor, and clean everybody's boots.

So off she had to go.

When she went in she had a good look at her stepmother, and sure enough she had a long nose, and she was as bony as a fish with all the flesh picked off, and the little girl thought of Baba Yaga and shivered, though she did not feel so bad when she remembered the mouseykin out there in the shed in the yard.

The very next morning it happened. The old man went off to pay a visit to some friends of his in the next village. And as soon as the old man was out of sight the wicked stepmother called the little girl.

'You are to go today to your dear little aunt in the forest,' says she, 'and ask her for a needle and thread to mend a shirt.'

'But here is a needle and thread,' said the little girl.

'Hold your tongue,' says the stepmother, and she gnashes her teeth, and they make a noise like clattering tongs. 'Hold your tongue,' she says. 'Didn't I tell you you are to go today to your dear little aunt to ask for a needle and thread to mend a shirt?'

'How shall I find her?' says the little girl, nearly ready to cry, for she knew that her aunt was Baba Yaga, the bony-legged, the witch.

The stepmother took hold of the little girl's nose and pinched it.

'That is your nose,' she says. 'Can you feel it?'

'Yes,' says the poor little girl.

'You must go along the road into the forest till you come to a fallen tree; then you must turn left, and then follow your nose and you will find her,' says the stepmother. 'Now, be off with you, lazy one. Here is some food for you to eat by the way.' She gave the little girl a bundle wrapped up in a towel.

The little girl wanted to go into the shed to tell the mouseykin she was going to Baba Yaga, and to ask what she should do. But she looked back, and there was the stepmother at the door watching her. So she had to go straight on.

She walked along the road through the forest till she came to the fallen tree. Then she turned to the left. Her nose was still hurting where the stepmother had pinched it, so she knew she had to go straight ahead. She was just setting out when she heard a little noise under the fallen tree.

Scratch. Scratch.

And out jumped the little mouse, and sat up in the road in front of her.

'O mouseykin, mouseykin,' says the little girl, 'my stepmother has sent me to her sister. And that is Baba Yaga, the bony-legged, the witch, and I do not know what to do.'

'It will not be difficult,' says the little mouse, 'because of your kind heart. Take all the things you find in the road, and do with them what you like. Then you will escape from Baba Yaga, and everything will be well.'

'Are you hungry, mouseykin?' said the little girl.

'I could nibble, I think,' says the little mouse.

The little girl unfastened the towel, and there was nothing in it but stones. That was what the stepmother had given the little girl to eat by the way.

'Oh, I'm so sorry,' says the little girl. 'There's nothing for you to eat.'

'Isn't there?' said mouseykin, and as she looked at them the little girl saw the stones turn to bread and jam. The little girl sat down on the fallen tree, and the little mouse sat beside her, and they ate bread and jam until they were not hungry any more.

'Keep the towel,' says the little mouse; 'I think it will be useful. And remember what I said about the things you find on the way. And now good-bye,' says he.

'Good-bye,' says the little girl, and runs along.

As she was running along she found a nice new handkerchief lying in the road. She picked it up and took it with her. Then she found a little bottle of oil. She picked it up and took it with her. Then she found some scraps of meat.

'Perhaps I'd better take them too,' she said; and she took them.

Then she found a gay blue ribbon, and she took that. Then she found a little loaf of good bread, and she took that too.

'I dare say somebody will like it,' she said.

And then she came to the hut of Baba Yaga, the bony-legged, the witch. There was a high fence round it with big gates. When she pushed them open they squeaked miserably, as if it hurt them to move. The little girl was sorry for them.

'How lucky,' she says, 'that I picked up the bottle of oil.' And she poured the oil into the hinges of the gates.

Inside the railing was Baba Yaga's hut, and it stood on hen's legs and walked about the yard. And in the yard there was standing Baba Yaga's servant, and she was crying bitterly because of the tasks Baba Yaga set her to do. She was crying bitterly and wiping her eyes on her petticoat.

'How lucky,' says the little girl, 'that I picked up a handkerchief.' And she gave the handkerchief to Baba Yaga's servant, who wiped her eyes on it and smiled through her tears.

Close by the hut was a huge dog, very thin, gnawing a dry crust.

'How lucky,' says the little girl, 'that I picked up a loaf.' And she gave the loaf to the dog, and he gobbled it up and licked his lips.

The little girl went bravely up to the hut and knocked on the door.

'Come in,' says Baba Yaga.

The little girl went in, and there was Baba Yaga, the bony-legged, the witch, sitting weaving at a loom. In a corner of the hut was a thin black cat watching a mousehole.

'Good day to you, auntie,' says the little girl, trying not to tremble.

'Good day to you, niece,' says Baba Yaga.

'My stepmother has sent me to ask for a needle and thread to mend a shirt.'

'Very well,' says Baba Yaga, smiling, and showing her iron

teeth. 'You sit down here at the loom, and go on with my weaving, while I go and get you the needle and thread.'

The little girl sat down at the loom and began to weave.

Baba Yaga went out and called to her servant, 'Go, make the bath hot, and scrub my niece. Scrub her clean. I'll make a dainty meal of her.'

The servant came in for the jug. The little girl begged her, 'Be not too quick in making the fire, and carry the water in a sieve.' The servant smiled but said nothing, because she was afraid of Baba Yaga. But she took a very long time about getting the bath ready.

Baba Yaga came to the window and asked:

'Are you weaving, little niece? Are you weaving, my pretty?'

'I am weaving, auntie,' says the little girl.

When Baba Yaga went away from the window, the little girl spoke to the thin black cat who was watching the mousehole.

'What are you doing, thin black cat?'

'Watching for a mouse,' says the thin black cat. 'I haven't had any dinner for three days.'

'How lucky,' says the little girl, 'that I picked up the scraps of meat.' And she gave them to the thin black cat. The thin black cat gobbled them up, and said to the little girl:

'Little girl, do you want to get out of this?'

'Catkin dear,' says the little girl, 'I do want to get out of this, for Baba Yaga is going to eat me with her iron teeth.'

'Well,' says the cat, 'I will help you.'

Just then Baba Yaga came to the window.

'Are you weaving, little niece?' she asked. 'Are you weaving, my pretty?'

'I am weaving, auntie,' says the little girl, working away, while the loom went clickety clack, clickety clack.

Baba Yaga went away.

Says the thin black cat to the little girl: 'You have a comb in your hair, and you have a towel. Take them and run for it, while Baba Yaga is in the bath-house. When Baba Yaga chases after you, you must listen; and when she is close to you throw away the towel, and it will turn into a big, wide river. It will take her a little time to get over that. But when she does, you must listen; and as soon as she is close to you throw away the comb, and it

92

will sprout up into such a forest that she will never get through it
at all.'

'But she'll hear the loom stop,' says the little girl.

'I'll see to that,' says the thin black cat.

The cat took the little girl's place at the loom.

Clickety clack, clickety clack; the loom never stopped for a
moment.

The little girl looked to see that Baba Yaga was in the bath-
house, and then she jumped down from the little hut on hen's
legs, and ran to the gates as fast as her legs could flicker.

The big dog leapt up to tear her to pieces. Just as he was going
to spring on her he saw who she was.

93

'Why, this is the little girl who gave me the loaf,' says he. 'A good journey to you, little girl,' and he lay down again with his head between his paws.

When she came to the gates they opened quietly, quietly, without making any noise at all, because of the oil she had poured into their hinges.

Outside the gates there was a little birch tree that beat her in the eyes so that she could not go by.

'How lucky,' says the little girl, 'that I picked up the ribbon.' And she tied up the birch tree with the pretty blue ribbon. And the birch tree was so pleased with the ribbon that it stood still, admiring itself, and let the little girl go by.

How she did run!

Meanwhile the thin black cat sat at the loom. Clickety clack, clickety clack, sang the loom; but you never saw such a tangle as the tangle made by the thin black cat.

And presently Baba Yaga came to the window.

'Are you weaving, little niece?' she asked. 'Are you weaving, my pretty?'

'I am weaving, auntie,' says the thin black cat, tangling and tangling, while the loom went clickety clack, clickety clack.

'That's not the voice of my little dinner,' says Baba Yaga, and she jumped into the hut, gnashing her iron teeth; and there was no little girl, but only the thin black cat, sitting at the loom, tangling and tangling the threads.

'Grr,' says Baba Yaga, and jumps for the cat, and begins banging it about. 'Why didn't you tear the little girl's eyes out?'

'In all the years I have served you,' says the cat, 'you have only given me one little bone; but the kind little girl gave me scraps of meat.'

Baba Yaga threw the cat into a corner, and went out into the yard.

'Why didn't you squeak when she opened you?' she asked the gates.

'Why didn't you tear her to pieces?' she asked the dog.

'Why didn't you beat her in the face, and not let her go by?' she asked the birch tree.

'Why were you so long in getting the bath ready? If you had

been quicker, she never would have got away,' said Baba Yaga to the servant.

And she rushed about the yard, beating them all, and scolding at the top of her voice.

'Ah!' said the gates, 'in all the years we have served you, you never eased us with water; but the kind little girl poured good oil into our hinges.'

'Ah!' said the dog, 'in all the years I've served you, you never threw me anything but burnt crusts; but the kind little girl gave me a good loaf.'

'Ah!' said the little birch tree, 'in all the years I've served you, you never tied me up, even with thread; but the kind little girl tied me up with a gay ribbon.'

'Ah!' said the servant, 'in all the years I've served you, you have never given me even a rag; but the kind little girl gave me a pretty handkerchief.'

Baba Yaga gnashed at them with her iron teeth. Then she jumped into the mortar and sat down. She drove it along with the pestle, and swept up her tracks with a besom, and flew off in pursuit of the little girl.

The little girl ran and ran. She put her ear to the ground and listened. Bang, bang, bangety bang! She could hear Baba Yaga beating the mortar with the pestle. Baba Yaga was quite close. There she was, beating with the pestle and sweeping with the besom, coming along the road.

As quickly as she could, the little girl took out the towel and threw it on the ground. And the towel grew bigger and bigger, and wetter and wetter, and there was a deep, broad river between Baba Yaga and the little girl.

The little girl turned and ran on. How she ran!

Baba Yaga came flying up in the mortar. But the mortar could not float in the river with Baba Yaga inside. She drove it in, but only got wet for her trouble. Tongs and pokers tumbling down a chimney are nothing to the noise she made as she gnashed her iron teeth. She turned home, and went flying back to the little hut on hen's legs. Then she got together all her cattle, and drove them to the river.

'Drink, drink!' she screamed at them; and the cattle drank up all the river to the last drop. And Baba Yaga, sitting in the mortar, drove it with the pestle, and swept up her tracks with the besom, and flew over the dry bed of the river in pursuit of the little girl.

The little girl put her ear to the ground and listened. Bang, bang, bangety bang! She could hear Baba Yaga beating the mortar with the pestle. Nearer and nearer came the noise, and there was Baba Yaga, beating with the pestle and sweeping with the besom, coming along the road close behind.

The little girl threw down the comb, and it grew bigger and bigger, and its teeth sprouted up into a thick forest, thicker than this forest where we live – so thick that not even Baba Yaga could force her way through. And Baba Yaga, gnashing her teeth and screaming with rage and disappointment, turned round and drove away home to her little hut on hen's legs.

The little girl ran on home. She was afraid to go in and see her stepmother, so she ran into the shed.

Scratch, scratch! Out came the little mouse.

'So you got away all right, my dear,' says the little mouse. 'Now run in. Don't be afraid. Your father is back, and you must tell him all about it.'

The little girl went into the house.

'Where have you been?' says her father, 'and why are you so out of breath?'

The stepmother turned yellow when she saw her, and her eyes glowed, and her teeth ground together until they broke.

But the little girl was not afraid, and she went to her father and climbed on his knee, and told him everything just as it had happened. And when the old man knew that the stepmother had sent his little daughter to be eaten by Baba Yaga, he was so angry that he drove her out of the hut, and ever afterwards lived alone with the little girl. Much better it was for both of them.

And the little mouse came and lived in the hut, and every day it used to sit up on the table and eat crumbs, and warm its paws on the little girl's glass of tea.

ARTHUR RANSOME

NUMBER TWELVE

Now this is a story of – *how many* people? ... Well, this is the way *I* tell it.

One day, twelve people went fishing. All friends.

There was Mandy and Sandy, and Jimmy and Timmy. That makes four. There was Poll and Moll, and Ted and Ned. That makes eight. And Bobby and Robby is ten, and Lindy and Cindy is twelve ... I *think*.

Hm, let me count them again. There was Lindy and Cindy and

Bobby and Robby. That makes four. And Poll and Moll and Ted and Ned. That makes eight. And Mandy and Timmy is ten, and Sandy and Jimmy is twelve . . . I *think*.

Well anyway, they all went fishing. And the sun shone, and the water of the river winked and flashed in the sun. Oh it was a glorious day for fishing!

Mandy caught a piece of wood.

Timmy caught a sausage tin.

Jimmy caught a boot.

Moll caught Cindy.

Poll caught a tree.

Ned caught the other side.

Cindy caught a man in a boat.

Ted caught Sandy.

Bobby caught a fantastic hat.

Robby caught a pram wheel.

Lindy caught Sandy.

Sandy caught herself.

Everyone caught something, so they were all very happy.

They went home talking and shouting and singing.

'I caught a shark in the sea!'

'I caught a thousand sharks!'

'I caught a whale in the sea!'

'I caught a million whales!'

'An octopus strangled me!'

'I strangled an octopus!'

'I'm Superman!'

'I'm Superwoman!'

'I nearly drowned!'

'*I* nearly drowned!'

'*We* nearly drowned *millions* of times!'

'How do you know if someone has drowned?' said Lindy.

'You just count,' said Ned, 'and if you're one short, then you know someone has drowned.'

They thought they had better make sure that no one had drowned. So they all got in a long line, and Ned stood in front of them, and walked down the line, counting.

'Lindy is one, Cindy is two, Mandy is three, Sandy is four, Jimmy is five, Timmy is six, Robby is seven, Bobby is eight, Poll is nine, Moll is ten, Ted is eleven, and –'

There was no one else there! Only eleven people! But there were twelve when they went out to fish.

They began to run about, looking for Number Twelve.

'Where are you, Number Twelve? Where are you?' But nobody answered.

After a bit, Poll said, 'Make a line again. I'll count.'

So they made a line again, and Poll counted.

'Ned is one and Ted is two. Sandy is three and Mandy is four. Jimmy is five and Timmy is six. Lindy is seven and Cindy is eight. Bobby is nine and Robby is ten. Moll is eleven and . . .'

There was no one else to count. Number Twelve had gone!

They were really scared. They ran about looking for Number Twelve. Somebody else counted, and then somebody else. But whoever counted – and in the end, *everybody* had a turn at counting – it always came to the same, eleven. No Number Twelve. But they certainly had Number Twelve when they started out.

'Somebody's drowned!' they cried to each other. 'Somebody's drowned!'

And they all ran back to the river, and ran along the bank, looking and calling and looking and calling, and back the way they came, looking and calling again.

But not a sign did they see of Number Twelve. So they began to cry, all of them.

While they were sitting in a heap, crying, a man came along.

'Whatever's the matter?' he said.

'We've lost Number Twelve, poor Number Twelve! Number Twelve's drowned,' they wailed.

'Really? Why do you say that?'

'We counted. We all counted. But there's no Number Twelve any more.'

'Now calm down,' he said (for the noise was tremendous). 'Just count again for me.'

So Cindy counted. Everyone got in a line, and Cindy walked along it, counting. And it came to eleven.

'Yes, you're right,' said the man. 'I see. I shall have to think very hard about this. You're rather lucky I came along, you know. I *think*, I really do *think*, that I *might* be able to find Number Twelve for you. But what will you give me if I do?'

'Oh, everything we've got, everything!' And they turned out their pockets on the spot, and gave him everything that was in them. They did want to see dear Number Twelve again.

'Right!' said the man. 'Stand in a line, everyone.' And he took a stick, and counted each one of them, and tapped each head with the stick as he counted.

'There's one. There's two. There's three. There's four. There's five. There's six, There's seven. There's eight. There's nine. There's ten. There's eleven.'

And when he got to twelve – because of course there *were* twelve of them when they were all together in one line – he gave that one an extra hard bonk on the head.

'THERE'S NUMBER TWELVE!' he shouted.

They were so excited! So pleased! So thankful! They all rushed up to Number Twelve.

'You're back! How lovely to see you! We thought we'd never find you again! Let me give you a hug! Let me give you a kiss! Where have you *been*?' Then they all, all of them, shouted together, 'Yes, where have you *been*?'

And Number Twelve, who was still quite dazed from the thump, said, 'Me? I don't think I've been anywhere.'

100

'Don't be so silly. You *must* have been somewhere or we couldn't have found you,' they said. 'Wasn't it lucky we did?'

And they all went home, the twelve of them ... Or eleven ... Or was it thirteen? ... Hm.

> *Snip snap snover,*
> That *tale's over.*

LEILA BERG

DAD'S LORRY

Tom's Dad had a big lorry. It was green, with enormous wheels and fat black tyres. At the front of the lorry was the cab where Tom's Dad sat when he was driving. He was so high up that he could look down on the cars and small vans on the road.

The back of the lorry was open and it had a tail-board at the back which Tom's Dad let down every time he loaded or unloaded. Across the side of the lorry was written,

THOMAS BUCKTON. HAULAGE CONTRACTOR. PHONE 7618.

(because Tom's Dad was called Tom too!)

The lorry was kept in a yard at the side of Tom's house and he was very proud of it. He liked to watch his Dad drive in and park so cleverly in such a small space or reverse out of the narrow entrance without even bumping the gates.

'When I grow up I'm going to drive Dad's lorry,' he told his friends. 'I shall drive for miles and miles and miles.'

Tom's Dad often had phone calls.

'Can you take a load of bricks to the building site next week?' someone at the brick works would ask.

'I need a load of cement tomorrow,' said the builder.

'I've a rush order on. Can you pick up some kitchen cupboards from the factory?' asked the carpenter.

It seemed as if everyone depended on Dad and his lorry to move things from one place to another.

'Oh dear. Bother that phone,' grumbled Mum sometimes, just when she had Tom's baby sister to bath and feed. 'It is always ringing when I am busy,'

But Dad just laughed. 'It's a good thing so many people do need my lorry,' he said. 'That's how I earn enough money to look after us all.'

During the week Tom's Dad drove off every morning after breakfast in the lorry. But on Saturdays he stayed at home. Tom thought it was the best day of the week. He always helped Dad to clean the lorry. They swept out the back and Tom loved it when he was lifted up there. It was like being up in an aeroplane because he could see over the fences into other people's gardens and into the street where the traffic went by.

After they had washed the lorry with a hose-pipe it looked really smart.

Now every Saturday afternoon Dad put on his best trousers and sweater and Mum put the baby in the push chair and they all went off into town to do their shopping. They bought groceries, meat, vegetables, bread and fruit from the supermarket, and if they had enough money left they went to a café and had hamburgers or sausage and chips.

Saturday was a SUPER day.

But one weekend Tom was looking forward especially to their shopping trip. It was the first weekend in December and Mum had promised him they would go to town and do some Christmas shopping. Their next-door neighbour had offered to look after the baby. 'With all those parcels to carry and crowds of Christmas shoppers,' she said, 'it will be no place for a pram and a baby.'

'It is going to be a lovely Christmas this year,' said Mum, with a dreamy look in her eye. 'It will be baby's first Christmas and Grandma and Grandad are coming from London to stay with us.'

'And I'll buy their Christmas presents with my pocket money,' said Tom, 'and something for the baby.'

However, just when they were all sitting down to breakfast on Saturday morning the phone rang.

'Oh dear,' they heard Dad say. 'Yes. I'll be very pleased to help you out. Yes. Yes I'll be sure and have my lorry there by one o'clock.'

He put the phone down.

'Sorry. I shan't be able to come Christmas shopping with you after all,' he said. 'I've an emergency job on. A very special job,'

Mum looked surprised. She knew Dad never worked on Saturdays. It sounded as if someone was in trouble and needed the lorry.

Tom was upset. 'But it won't be the same without you, Dad,' he said crossly. He couldn't understand it at all. Dad didn't even look disappointed. In fact he was almost smiling, and Tom pushed his toast round and round the plate instead of eating it.

'Why did someone have to want Dad's lorry just on this particular Saturday?' he muttered to himself.

Dad drove off in his lorry at midday, waving and calling cheerily, 'Have a good time in town, Tom. There'll be lots of traffic about so look after Mum, won't you?'

Tom nodded gloomily and went off to fetch his pocket money ready to buy Christmas presents for Grandma and Grandad and his baby sister. But he didn't feel happy at all.

The shops were crowded with people all doing their Christmas shopping and Mum was very glad to have Tom's help to carry a big plastic bag. Crackers, decorations for the Christmas cake, nuts, mincemeat, a packet of stuffing for the turkey and silver balls to hang on the tree – they all went into the plastic bag.

Tom began to feel excited. Christmas would soon be here. He found a mobile to hang in his little sister's room with shiny silver stars on it. She would love that for a present, and a pen for Grandad and pink handkerchiefs for Grandma were just the very thing.

'Oh dear!' Mum looked very tired. 'That is as much shopping as I can do today.' She looked at her watch. 'Half past three. Time for a special treat now, Tom. Come along. We'll go over to Barclay's Store across the road. Father Christmas is due to arrive there at four o'clock.'

'Father Christmas!' cried Tom. 'You didn't tell me he was coming this afternoon.'

Mum laughed. 'He is coming to open the "Fairy Grotto" and I

wanted it to be a surprise for you,' she said. 'A nice ending to our Christmas shopping trip '

When they arrived outside the store there was no doubt something very exciting was about to happen. The police had stopped all the traffic and the pavements were crowded with people. But Tom and his Mum were lucky and found a place to stand just near the main entrance where Father Christmas would be entering the store.

'You stand here in front of us,' said a friendly old gentleman and his wife. 'You'll be able to see everything here,' and moving up close together they made a space for Tom and his Mum.

It was all very exciting. People were laughing and talking and the children were waving and jumping about and looking up the road to see if Father Christmas was coming. One kind policeman leaned over and put a tiny girl on his shoulders so she would be able to see better.

Tom did wish his Dad was there because he loved treats like this. The Christmas lights which decorated the shops and which were strung across the road shone and twinkled in the early winter dusk, and two big Christmas trees stood on either side of the entrance to the store. They were covered with tinsel and fairy lights. The street looked really wonderful.

One lady pointed to the big clock outside the store. 'Four o'clock. He'll soon be here,' she said. And just then, away in the distance Tom could hear music.

> *Rudolph the red-nosed reindeer,*
> *Had a very shiny nose.*

'He's coming Mum,' he cried. 'Father Christmas. Look!'

Everyone began to cheer and shout. The policemen were busy keeping the road clear for Father Christmas and along came a

lorry. It was strung all over with fairy lights and decorated with holly and branches of greenery. Two big flood lights on the sides lit up a tall red chimney, and there, standing beside the chimney, was jolly Father Christmas, with a flowing white beard, a red hood and cloak and carrying an enormous sack on his shoulder.

He was waving to the children as the music played,

Jingle bells. Jingle bells.

BUT TOM WAS NOT EVEN LOOKING AT FATHER CHRISTMAS.

'Mum,' he shouted above the noise. 'It's Dad's lorry ... and it's DAD DRIVING!'

By this time Mum was getting as excited as Tom. 'It is. It's Dad in his lorry and he is driving Father Christmas. So *that's* the special job he had to do, and he kept it a secret so we could have a wonderful surprise.'

Tom shouted to the old lady and gentleman who had helped them to find such a good place to stand.

'It's my Dad. Look, he's driving Father Christmas in his lorry.'

By this time the lorry had stopped – just outside the entrance to the store where Tom and his Mum were and Dad peeped out of the cab and winked at them.

'How's that then?' he called. 'You didn't expect to see *me* with Father Christmas, did you?'

Tom had never felt so proud in his life. Whatever would his friends at school say when he told them?

The manager of the store, looking very important, was waiting to help Father Christmas down from the back of the lorry.

'We are very pleased to welcome you to our store today, Father Christmas,' he said. 'Will you please come and open our Fairy Grotto?'

Father Christmas waved to everyone. 'Happy Christmas, children,' he called. 'Come and see me in the Fairy Grotto. I shall be waiting there with some presents for you all.'

Then ... just as he was about to go in through the big entrance door, he turned and hurried back to the lorry. Reaching up he shook Tom's Dad by the hand and said, so loudly that all the people standing round could hear, 'My lorry broke down this morning and I was very worried about how I should get here. I

don't know what I should have done without your lorry. Thank you for all your help.'

'It was a pleasure, Father Christmas,' said Tom's Dad, looking very pleased with himself indeed.

Mum and Tom decided they would come back another day when there were not so many people around and see the Fairy Grotto then. They were so excited that all they really wanted to do was hurry home as fast as they could and hear all that Dad had to tell them about his adventure.

They carried all the shopping home, talking all the time, and just had time to get the tea ready when they heard a 'Honk, honk,' and Dad came driving into the yard, lights blazing and pieces of holly still hanging on the sides of the lorry.

Tom and his Mum hugged Dad. 'Who's got an early Christmas present?' he said, laughing and handing Tom a parcel all wrapped up in Christmas paper. 'And one for the baby too,' he said. 'Father Christmas gave them to me.'

'This really must be the most exciting Saturday ever,' Tom thought when he opened his parcel and saw a police car – just what he wanted to add to his collection of small cars. The baby had a plastic ball with a bell inside which tinkled as it rolled along. She would love that.

It didn't seem possible that anything else exciting could happen to add to the wonderful day. But do you know, there was one more surprise before Tom went to bed!

Tom's Dad turned on the television to get the News and there – right on their own television set – was a picture of Tom's Dad driving his lorry down the main street of the town, lights blazing, music playing and Father Christmas waving to all the people. And when Tom looked very carefully, there standing by the main entrance to the store, he could just see Mum and HIMSELF, jumping up and down and pointing to Dad.

'Everyone seems to need Dad's lorry,' thought Tom, as he went off to sleep that night, 'even Father Christmas.'

PHYLLIS PEARCE

GOAT COMES TO THE CHRISTMAS PARTY

'Hurry! Hurry! Hurry!' said Gran'ma to Araminta. 'It's time to go to the party.'

'Hurry! Hurry! Hurry!' said Araminta to Jerome Anthony. 'It's time to go to the party.'

Christmas had come to the country, and there was going to be a party at the schoolhouse. Everybody was going, so Araminta and Jerome Anthony and Gran'ma had to hurry, else they'd be late and miss something.

'I wish Goat could go to the party,' said Araminta, shaking her head sadly. 'It seems a shame that Goat can't have any Christmas at all.'

'Goats don't have Christmas,' laughed Jerome Anthony. 'What ever would Goat do at a party?'

'Hurry! Hurry! Hurry!' said Gran'ma, looking at her watch.

So they put on their hats and coats and mittens. They tied their scarves under their chins, and they started out. It was cold, so

they walked fast and it didn't take any time to get to the school-house. If they hadn't hurried they might have been late, for the party was just about to begin.

Everyone was there sitting on the school benches that were pushed back against the wall of the room. The beautiful paper chains and popcorn strings were there on the Christmas tree just where they belonged. And over in one corner was a table filled with cakes and lemonade and candy, for of course a party isn't a party without good things to eat.

'Where is Gran'pa?' asked Jerome Anthony, turning around in his seat. 'I'm afraid Gran'pa is going to be late.'

'Don't you worry,' said Gran'ma, smiling. 'Gran'pa will get here. He has a surprise for you.'

'Surprise!' whispered Araminta, very excited. Then her face was sad. 'Oh dear, I do wish Goat could be here for the surprise.'

Just then there was a little noise at the back door and everyone turned around. Well, you can't imagine what they saw! Santa

Claus! There he was in a red suit with white trimmings, and a red cap with a white tassel. And he had the reddest face you've ever seen, with a long white beard at the bottom of it.

'Oh! Oh!' yelled everybody.

'Shh-h-h!' whispered everybody.

For Santa Claus had somebody with him. This somebody was black and white with long floppy ears and a short stumpy tail. This somebody had long curly horns that looked very much like the branches of a tree. This somebody was hitched to a new green wagon. Yes, you've guessed it, Santa Claus had a reindeer with him, and this reindeer was pulling a wagon full of toys!

'Oh! Oh! Oh!' yelled everybody.

'Shh-h-h!' whispered everybody.

For Santa Claus and the reindeer were starting up the aisle towards the Christmas tree. They walked along steadily until they came to a bench where Jerome Anthony and Araminta were sitting, and then something very queer happened. That reindeer lifted his stumpy tail; he shook his head and his ears went flip-flop.

'GOAT!' yelled Araminta, jumping up and down. 'Goat has come to the party!'

We can't be sure whether it was Araminta yelling or the sight of the Christmas tree, but anyway, just then Santa Claus's

reindeer stopped acting like a reindeer and began acting like a goat instead. He butted Santa Claus out of the way. He broke loose from his wagon. He began *eating* the Christmas tree!

'Hey! Watch out!' said Santa Claus, falling against one of the benches. When he got up, that red face with the long white beard had fallen off.

'Gran'pa!' yelled Jerome Anthony. 'Gran'pa got here after all!'

We can't be sure whether it was Jerome Anthony yelling or the sight of that goat eating the Christmas tree, but anyway, Santa Claus stopped acting like Santa Claus and began to act like Gran'pa instead. He grabbed hold of Goat. But every time he tried to stop Goat eating the popcorn off the tree, Goat reared up and butted him against the benches again.

'Let me help,' said Araminta, jumping up. 'I can manage that Goat.'

She grabbed Goat by his bridle and started to lead him away before he ruined the tree. But just then Goat caught sight of the table full of cakes and candy and lemonade, and he pulled towards that.

Now when goats see something that they want to eat, you know how hard it is to keep them away from it. Araminta pulled and pulled, but it didn't do any good. Goat kept on getting closer and closer to that table of good food.

'Oh! Oh! Oh!' everybody yelled. They didn't want all their party refreshments to be eaten up.

'Shh-h-h!' everybody whispered, because it looked as if Jerome Anthony was going to do something about it.

He took two pieces of chocolate cake from the table and he held them out to Goat.

'Here, Goat!' he said.

Goat looked at the cake held out for him to eat; he reared up on his hind legs and shook those pretend reindeer horns off his short horns; then he ran after Jerome Anthony! Jerome Anthony ran down the middle of the schoolhouse, holding that cake so Goat could see it. Goat ran after him.

'Humph!' said Araminta, taking a deep breath, 'I shouldn't have worried about Goat not having any Christmas. He had more than anybody else.'

Gran'pa put on his red face with the white whiskers and there he was – a Santa Claus again. 'Merry Christmas!' he laughed as he began to give out the toys. 'Merry Christmas!' yelled everybody.

'Maa-aa! Maa-a-a!' came Goat's voice from the schoolhouse yard.

But nobody opened the door to let him in.

EVA KNOX EVANS

COLD FEET

Once upon a time, there were a King and Queen. Most of the time, they were very happy. The only trouble was that the King was terribly untidy – he would keep leaving his clothes all over the palace.

'If you leave ANY more clothes lying around,' said the Queen one morning, as she picked up a jumper, some hats and a coat off

111

the bedroom floor, 'or lose your socks again – I'll – I'll – I won't make any more special fruit cake for tea!' And she stormed out.

'Oh dear,' said the King to himself, 'I'd better not tell her I've lost my crown and my socks. I couldn't go without my fruit cake. I wonder where the crown can be?'

And he sat down on his throne, to have a think.

'Ow!' The King leapt up again – and looked at his throne. There was his crown.

'Well, at least I've found *that!*' He put the crown on his head, and sat back on the throne. 'Now where have I left my socks?'

He thought and thought. It was no good. He couldn't even think where he'd left one sock.

He hunted all round the royal bedroom – under the bed, inside

the chest, on top of the wardrobe, even all through his dirty clothes. Not one sock to be found.

'Dear oh dear!' said the King. 'I dare not tell the Queen I've lost them. I shall have to think of a reason for not wearing them, that's all.'

Then he had an idea. 'I know! I'll issue a proclamation – that's what kings do when they're in a spot of trouble.'

Next day, all over the palace there were large notices, proclaiming: 'NO SOCKS TO BE WORN IN THIS PALACE FOR A WEEK. SIGNED – THE KING.'

People were rather surprised, but if the King told them to take off their socks, then take them off they must. So, for a week, everyone in the palace, and everyone who came to the palace, went barefoot.

At the end of the week, the King, very pleased with his idea, was getting ready to write out a new proclamation to carry on for another week, when the Queen came in looking tearful over a large bundle of assorted socks.

'Something the matter, dear?' asked the King, as he signed his name with a flourish.

'It's all these socks,' said the Queen, shaking her head. 'Everybody who's come to visit the palace this week – the milkman, the postman, the baker, the King of Belgravia and his son – they've all had to take their socks off, and leave them in a pile on the doorstep. But the socks always get mixed up, and they all look alike – nobody can find their own! So they keep going home barefoot.'

'Never mind, my dear,' said the King, 'at least the sock-maker in town will have a lot of work making new socks for everyone . . . Now I'll just go and get this new proclamation printed . . .'

But at that moment, there was a knock at the palace door.

'I'll get it,' said the Queen. 'I expect it's the postman.'

She came back in a few moments with a letter and a large parcel. 'They're for you,' she said handing them to the King.

'I'll leave the parcel till last,' he said, opening the letter. 'Well, well, well! What a surprise! It's from Fred Bonker – Maker of Best Quality Socks!'

'Is he pleased with the work he's been getting?' asked the Queen.

'Well, he says: "Your Majesty, I have been making socks night and day for the last week and I am VERY TIRED. Please will you cancel your proclamation, and let everyone keep their socks on again, because I need a rest." Signed, "Fred Bonker, Sock Maker." '

'Poor man,' said the Queen. 'You will cancel the proclamation, won't you?'

'No, no!' said the King hurriedly. 'I couldn't possibly.' And he quickly opened the parcel. He couldn't believe his eyes. It was a box full of socks – different colours, different patterns, some short and some long.

'By jove!' said the King. 'These are rather nice – much nicer than any of the ones I lost – I mean, than any of the ones I'm not wearing at the moment.'

'They're from Fred Bonker,' said the Queen, reading the note which was inside. 'He hopes you'll like them so much, you'll want to keep them on your feet and cancel the proclamation.'

'Splendid!' said the King, beaming from ear to ear. 'I'll wear this pair today, and that pair tomorrow . . .'

'But what about the proclamation?'

'Oh, cancel the proclamation!' said the King.

'Hurray!' said the Queen. 'I'll make some fruit cake for tea to celebrate.' And she rushed off to the kitchen.

The King tried on a pair of his new socks. 'Wonderful!' he exclaimed, wiggling his toes. 'It's going to take me a very long time to lose all these!' And he tore up his proclamation and went off to the kitchen to wait for the fruit cake.

SUSAN EAMES

THE CLOWN PRINCE

Once there was a Prince who was very unhappy; nothing ever made him laugh or smile. No matter how many clowns or minstrels the King brought to the palace, the Prince just sat sadly sighing.

They tried everything to brighten him up: circuses from far-off places, acrobats, parties and dances, but the Prince's face remained sad and glum. The King and the court all loved the Prince, and as he became more unhappy, so did they.

The people of the country also grew sad when they heard how unhappy their Prince was. Soon the whole country was very quiet and sad. No one sang or danced, and the children forgot how to play.

When the Prince saw he was making everyone unhappy, he decided to go away, so one day he rode off. Across the land,

through cities and villages he travelled, looking for happiness, but he found only sadness in the land.

Finally he came to a dark forest. 'This place looks as unhappy as I am,' he thought as he rode through it. Soon he came upon a very old man sitting by a statue of a girl. The old man told the Prince that the statue was really his daughter, who had long ago been turned into stone by a wicked witch and could only come alive again when everyone in the land smiled and was happy.

When the Prince saw how beautiful the stone girl was his heart sank. 'Everyone is unhappy in the land,' he sighed, 'and it is all because of me. How can people find happiness?'

'That is no secret,' said the old man. 'To be happy yourself you must make others happy.'

The Prince had never thought of this because he had expected other people to make him happy, so he decided to try it, there and then.

He took off his princely robes and tried to make the careworn old man smile. The Prince looked so odd, tumbling around with his long, sad face that the old man soon smiled and laughed as he had not done for many years. Glancing at the statue, the Prince saw tiny cracks around the girl's mouth where the stone was trying to smile.

The Prince felt a thrill in his heart. 'I see how to make others happy,' he said. 'I will go through the land until all the people smile, but I shall never be happy until your daughter is real again, because I love her.'

The Prince went off, telling the old man he would return when he had broken the spell. On his journey he charmed the animals of the forest with his antics, and sang such tunes that long after he had gone the animals were still singing them and playing in the sun.

The Prince went into villages full of sad people; with his tricks and antics and his long, sad face, he looked so strange that soon everyone was laughing at him, and when they had remembered how to laugh, the Prince played such games and sung such wonderful songs that the people became happy again and laughed whenever they thought of him.

The Prince loved to see the people happy, but he did not feel the same thrill as when the statue had tried to smile.

As he went through the country his fame spread. Whole towns came to see him and went away singing and dancing. He wore strange clothes and taught others how to clown and jest, but no one could look as funny as the Prince with his long, sad face.

So the country became the happiest place in the world. When everyone was happy and smiling the Clown Prince thought, 'Now the statue will be real.'

He went back to the forest and found the old man still sitting by the statue.

'Why is she still stone?' asked the Prince.

The old man shook his head and said, 'There must be one person in the land who is still unhappy.'

The Prince went searching for the unhappy person. He travelled far and wide, but found only happiness; then he received a summons to the palace, to make the King laugh.

When he arrived he realized it was the King who was keeping the spell from being broken, because he was sad. Yet no amount of the clown's antics could cheer him up.

'Why are you so sad, King?' he asked.

'Because my son the unhappy Prince has never returned,' the King told the clown. Then the Clown Prince took off his hood and the make-up from his face, and showed the King who he really was; that made the King very happy. So the Prince went back again to the forest. He found the old man, and the statue. But the beautiful girl was still locked in stone.

'Why is she still a statue?' the Prince cried to the old man. 'I've made everyone in the kingdom smile.'

'There must still be one who isn't smiling,' the old man said.

The Prince wandered through the forest. 'Who can he be?' he thought, and sat by a lake to think. The Prince then saw his own reflection in the water: his solemn, sad face stared at him.

'It's me,' he cried. 'I am the only one who has never smiled, because I couldn't be happy until the spell was broken.'

So the Prince laughed at himself and broke the spell. Rushing back, he found the statue cracking and becoming a real girl.

The Prince took her and her father home. The King married them and they lived in the happiest land in the world.

If ever anyone was sad, the Prince would put on his clown's clothes and his long face, and soon had them laughing again. So he became known as the Clown Prince.

MALCOLM CARRICK

ELEPHANT BIG AND ELEPHANT LITTLE

Elephant Big was always boasting.

'I'm bigger and better than you,' he told Elephant Little. 'I can run faster, and shoot water higher out of my trunk, and eat more, and . . .'

'No, you can't!' said Elephant Little.

Elephant Big was surprised. Elephant Big was *always* right. Then he curled up his trunk and laughed and laughed.

'What's more, I'll show you,' said Elephant Little. 'Let's have a running race, and a shooting-water-out-of-our-trunks race, and an eating race. We'll soon see who wins.'

'I shall, of course,' boasted Elephant Big. 'Lion shall be judge.'

'The running race first!' Lion said. 'Run two miles there and two miles back. One of you runs in the field, the other one runs in the forest. Elephant Big shall choose.'

Elephant Big thought and thought, and Elephant Little pretended to talk to himself: 'I hope he chooses to run in the field, because *I* want to run in the forest.'

When Elephant Big heard this, he thought: 'If Elephant Little wants very much to run in the forest, that means the forest is best.' Aloud he said: 'I choose the forest.'

'Very well,' said Lion. 'One, two, three, go!'

Elephant Little had short legs, but they ran very fast on the springy smooth grass of the field. Elephant Big had long, strong legs, but they could not carry him quickly along through the forest. Broken branches lay in his way; thorns tore at him; tangled grass caught at his feet. By the time he stumbled, tired and panting, back to the winning post, Elephant Little had run his four miles, and was standing talking to Lion.

'What ages you've been!' said Elephant Little. 'We thought you were lost.'

'Elephant Little wins,' said Lion.

Elephant Little smiled to himself.

'But I'll win the next race,' said Elephant Big. 'I can shoot water much higher than you can.'

'All right!' said Lion. 'One of you fills his trunk from the river, the other fills his trunk from the lake. Elephant Big shall choose.'

Elephant Big thought and thought, and Elephant Little pretended to talk to himself: 'I hope he chooses the river, because *I* want to fill my trunk from the lake.'

When Elephant Big heard this, he thought: 'If Elephant Little wants very much to fill his trunk from the lake, that means the lake is best.' Aloud he said: 'I choose the lake.'

'Very well!' said Lion. 'One, two, three, go!'

Elephant Little ran to the river and filled his trunk with clear, sparkling water. His trunk was small, but he spouted the water as high as a tree.

Elephant Big ran to the lake, and filled his long, strong trunk with water. But the lake water was heavy with mud, and full of slippery, tickly fishes. When Elephant Big spouted it out, it rose only as high as a middle-sized thorn bush. He lifted his trunk and tried harder than ever. A cold little fish slipped down his throat, and Elephant Big spluttered and choked.

'Elephant Little wins,' said Lion.

Elephant Little smiled to himself.

When Elephant Big stopped coughing, he said: 'But I'll win the next race, see if I don't. I can eat much more than you can.'

'Very well!' said Lion. 'Eat where you like and how you like.'

Elephant Big thought and thought, and Elephant Little pretended to talk to himself: 'I must eat and eat as fast as I can, and I mustn't stop; not for a minute.'

Elephant Big thought to himself: 'Then I must do exactly the same. I must eat and eat as fast as I can, and I mustn't stop; not for a minute.'

'Are you ready?' asked Lion. 'One, two, three, go!'

Elephant Big bit and swallowed, and bit and swallowed, as fast as he could, without stopping. Before very long, he began to feel full up inside.

Elephant Little bit and swallowed, and bit and swallowed. Then

he stopped eating and ran round a thorn bush three times. He felt perfectly well inside.

Elephant Big went on biting and swallowing, biting and swallowing, without stopping. He began to feel very, very funny inside.

Elephant Little bit and swallowed, and bit and swallowed. Then again he stopped eating, and ran round a thorn bush six times. He felt perfectly well inside.

Elephant Big bit and swallowed, and bit and swallowed, as fast as he could, without stopping once, until he felt so dreadfully ill inside that he had to sit down.

Elephant Little had just finished running around a thorn bush nine times, and he still felt perfectly well inside. When he saw Elephant Big on the ground, holding his tummy and groaning horribly, Elephant Little smiled to himself.

'Oh, I do like eating, don't you?' he said. 'I've only just started. I could eat and eat and eat and eat.'

'Oh, oh, oh!' groaned Elephant Big.

'Why, what's the matter?' asked Elephant Little. 'You look queer. Sort of green! When are you going to start eating again?'

'Not a single leaf more!' groaned Elephant Big. 'Not a blade of grass, not a twig can I eat!'

'Elephant Little wins,' said Lion.

Elephant Big felt too ill to speak.

After that day, if Elephant Big began to boast, Elephant Little smiled, and said: 'Shall we have a running race? Shall we spout water? Or shall we just eat and eat and eat?'

Then Elephant Big would remember. Before very long, he was one of the nicest, most friendly elephants ever to take a mud bath.

ANITA HEWETT

ALPHA BETA
AND GRANDMA DELTA

Do you want to know what made big, handsome Alpha Beta, dog-with-a-bark-that-could-be-heard-in-the-next-street, angrier than anything?

Grandma Delta, old Grandma Delta cat, with twenty-three children and one hundred and twenty-one grandchildren, could leap up and over the garden fence, could leap any fence she met and *go wherever she liked*. Alpha Beta walked around the garden. Fence at the end, fence at each side, house and gate to the front, lawn in the middle, with one tree. He knew it all. There was

no way out for a dog. Same grass, same plants and same tree, every day.

Alpha Beta looked up at Grandma Delta lying relaxed along the branch of a tree. He growled. Grandma Delta flicked her tail. 'How dare that cat sit in the tree?' thought Alpha Beta. There was no chance of reaching her. And she looked comfortable.

Grandma Delta was bored with the tree. She sprang down, ran along the path, leapt on to the top of the fence, balanced – then with one long leap she reached the upstairs window-sill at the side

125

of the house. The window-sill was warm in the sun. Grandma Delta curled up and went to sleep.

Alpha Beta growled with rage. How dare that cat! He ran around the garden and back. Round the tree. *Bark! Bark!* He ran the other way round the tree. What was the use? Alpha Beta lay down, not looking at Grandma Delta, and pretended to sleep. Grandma Delta had not moved. High up on the window-sill she could see about three gardens at once, if she wanted to.

Alpha Beta sighed. What was on the other side of the fence? He could not see through the fence, nor over it. He could only hear noises, and smell the smells. Alpha Beta dozed in the sun.

A sudden click woke him. Grandma Delta had padded past without him noticing and leapt up the fence. She paused, and was gone.

Alpha Beta put his nose in the air and howled with despair.

Something touched him on the paw. Alpha Beta looked through his howls and saw the most beautiful Fairy Dog.

'Oh, Alpha Beta,' said the Fairy Dog. 'I have come to grant you your wish.'

'Let me do what that cat can do,' breathed Alpha Beta.

'I will grant you your wish,' said the Fairy Dog. 'But you can only un-wish it three times.'

And she was gone.

Alpha Beta stood still. Thank goodness the Fairy Dog had not changed him into a cat! That would be terrible. But could he really do what a cat can do? Did he dare?

Alpha Beta looked up at the tree. He rushed at the trunk and threw his paws at it. A miracle! They held to the bark. He clambered up – up – to the branch where Grandma Delta always sat. It worked.

He felt dizzy with joy. Then he looked down. No, don't do that. Alpha Beta lay along the branch of the tree. The branch moved with the wind. Alpha Beta clung on tighter. The branch swayed, the light jigged between the leaves, and the ground looked a long way down. 'I'm doing it, I'm doing it,' chanted Alpha Beta to himself. 'Just let Grandma Delta come back and she will see that I am here instead of her.'

He held on a little tighter. 'But I think that is probably enough for the first day and I'll get down now.'

How? Suddenly Alpha Beta could not remember how Grandma Delta got down out of the tree. Front first? Not possible! Jump? It was too far. He edged himself along the branch towards the trunk. Perhaps the back legs first? But he didn't feel like letting go. The branch seemed very narrow and thin. 'Oh, help!' cried Alpha Beta. 'I wish I was back on the ground.'

And he was.

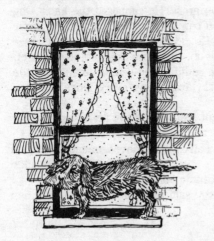

That was much better. Good old ground. It did not sway about. 'Just lack of practice,' said Alpha Beta to himself. 'That is the only problem, but I don't think I will go back up into the tree at the moment. I know,' thought Alpha Beta, 'the window-sill! That can't move. It will be much better. I should have tried it first.'

As soon as he got up on the window-sill Alpha

Beta knew it was a mistake. The sill was far too narrow. It was terrible. 'Help!' called Alpha Beta, forgetting everything except how frightened he was. 'Get me *down*.'

And he was.

'Never, never, never again,' said Alpha Beta.

But how silly he was being. The really important thing was the fence. Now he could get out. At long last he, Alpha Beta dog, could get over the fence and see what lay beyond.

Alpha Beta stood back. Then he ran a few steps forwards, leapt, clung briefly half-way up the fence – another leap up – balance on the top – and he was over.

The first thing Alpha Beta noticed was another fence. It looked like the one he had just come over. In fact everything looked rather the same. He was in another garden. There was a fence at the bottom, a fence at each side, grass, a tree. Alpha Beta was just going to inspect the bottom of the garden when there was a most awful noise.

'There's a dog! A dog in the garden! That dog from next door has got into our garden. Get him out!'

The shouts came louder, closer. Things were being thrown at him.

'Oh, get me out of here!' cried Alpha Beta. 'I wish I was back home.' And he was.

Alpha Beta dog lay on the grass. He supposed the Fairy Dog meant it when she said, 'You can only un-wish your wish three times.' But he did not mind. He did not want to even try and see if he could do what a cat can do. Grandma Delta could dance on the roof for all he cared. She could swing upside down from the top of the tree, or walk backwards along every fence. He was staying where he was.

But Grandma Delta had not seen one of the awful things that had happened. And that was all that mattered.

MEREDITH HOOPER

DID I EVER TELL YOU ABOUT THE TIME WHEN I BIT A BOY CALLED DANNY PAYNE?

When I first started school we all sat at little desks. There were six children in each row. We kept our books and crayons in cardboard boxes which the teacher called Tidy Boxes.

One of the children who sat by my desk was a boy called Danny Payne. He stole the best crayons from our Tidy Boxes. He made dirty smudges on our work. The worst thing Danny Payne did was to pinch us.

Whenever Miss White, the teacher, wasn't looking he pinched us on our arms, our hands, our chests and our backs. When Miss White was looking Danny Payne would stick his horrible dirty hands under the desk and pinch us on our thighs.

In the playground Danny Payne was just as bad. He kicked and punched and tripped children over. We all tried to keep away from him.

Nobody wanted to sit next to him in the classroom. We all waited until Danny Payne sat down. Then we would rush to sit as far away from him as possible. The last two children shoved their chairs as far away as possible.

Even when we sat as far away as possible from Danny Payne, his arms would reach under the desk to pinch us. He was an expert pincher. In the playground we would show each other the little black bruises Danny Payne had made.

One day Danny Payne kept pinching my friend Margaret. Her legs were covered in black bruises. Margaret went to the front of the classroom to tell Miss White. But Miss White didn't listen. She told Margaret to sit down and get on with her writing.

Graham, Susie and I put our heads together. We decided we

would all go to tell Miss White about Danny Payne and about the bruises all over Margaret's legs.

Miss White looked up from her desk. She said a really stupid thing. 'If it's a tale, go and tie a knot in it.' Of course she meant 'tale' like a story, not 'tail' like an animal has. So we all sat down again. You can't tie knots in stories.

Then Danny Payne started pinching us for trying to tell tales about him. He pinched me on my arm. He pinched Graham on his neck and he pinched Susie a mighty pinch right on her bottom.

Danny Payne was impossible! I grabbed his arm and buried my teeth into the back of his wrist. I kept on biting until he screamed.

Miss White had to take notice this time. Danny Payne threw himself down on the floor. He screamed and screamed and screamed. When Miss White picked him up he sobbed and sobbed. 'Poor Danny,' said Miss White.

Miss White took us both to the headmistress, Mrs Musselbrook. 'Poor Danny,' said Mrs Musselbrook when she saw my teethmarks in his wrist, 'you're a wicked, cruel girl,' she squawked.

Then she gave me a horrible punishment. Mrs Musselbrook went into the cloakroom and came back with a bar of soggy soap. She made me bite the soap to teach me not to bite poor little boys like Danny Payne.

This story has a happy ending. I was nearly sick from biting the

bar of soap, but Danny Payne never pinched anyone again, even though he still punched and kicked and tripped over children in the playground. I was glad I bit him.

IRIS GRENDER

MY NAUGHTY LITTLE SISTER AT THE PARTY

You wouldn't think there could be another child as naughty as my naughty little sister, would you? But there was. There was a thoroughly bad boy who was my naughty little sister's best boy-friend, and this boy's name was Harry.

This Bad Harry and my naughty little sister used to play together quite a lot in Harry's garden, or in our garden, and got up to dreadful mischief between them, picking all the baby gooseberries,

131

and the green blackcurrants, and throwing sand on the flower-beds, and digging up the runner-bean seeds, and all the naughty sorts of things you never, never do in the garden.

Now, one day this Bad Harry's birthday was near, and Bad Harry's mother said he could have a birthday-party and invite lots of children to tea. So Bad Harry came round to our house with a pretty card in an envelope for my naughty little sister, and this card was an invitation asking my naughty little sister to come to the birthday-party.

Bad Harry told my naughty little sister that there would be a lovely tea with jellies and sandwiches and birthday-cake, and my naughty little sister said, 'Jolly good.'

And every time she thought about the party she said, 'Nice tea and birthday-cake.' Wasn't she greedy? And when the party day came she didn't make any fuss when my mother dressed her in her new green party-dress, and her green party-shoes and her green hair-ribbon, and she didn't fidget and she didn't wriggle her head about when she was having her hair combed, she kept as still as still, because she was so pleased to think about the party, and when my mother said, 'Now, what must you say at the party?' my naughty little sister said, 'I must say, "nice tea".'

But my mother said, 'No, no, that would be a greedy thing to say. You must say "please" and "thank you" like a good polite child at tea-time, and say, "thank you very much for having me," when the party is over.'

And my naughty little sister said, 'All right, Mother, I promise.'

So my mother took my naughty little sister to the party, and what do you think the silly little girl did as soon as she got there? She went up to Bad Harry's mother and said very quickly, 'Please-and-thank-you, and-thank-you-very-much for-having-me,' all at once – just like that, before she forgot to be polite, and then she said, 'Now, may I have a lovely tea?'

Wasn't that rude and greedy? Bad Harry's mother said, 'I'm afraid you will have to wait until all the other children are here, but Harry shall show you the tea-table if you like.'

Bad Harry looked very smart in a blue party-suit, with white socks and shoes and a *real man's haircut*, and he said, 'Come on, I'll show you.'

So they went into the tea-room and there was the birthday-tea spread out on the table. Bad Harry's mother had made red jellies and yellow jellies, and blancmanges and biscuits and sandwiches and cakes-with-cherries-on, and a big birthday-cake with white icing on it and candles and 'Happy Birthday Harry' written on it.

My naughty little sister's eyes grew bigger and bigger, and Bad Harry said, 'There's something else in the larder. It's going to be a surprise treat, but you shall see it because you are my best girl-friend.'

So Bad Harry took my naughty little sister out into the kitchen and they took chairs and climbed up to the larder shelf – which is a dangerous thing to do, and it would have been their own faults if they had fallen down – and Bad Harry showed my naughty little sister a lovely spongy trifle, covered with creamy stuff and with silver balls and jelly-sweets on the top. And my naughty little sister stared more than ever because she liked spongy trifle better than jellies or blancmanges or biscuits or sandwiches or cakes-with-cherries-on, or even birthday-cake, so she said, 'For me.'

Bad Harry said, 'For me too,' because he liked spongy trifle best as well.

Then Bad Harry's mother called to them and said, 'Come along, the other children are arriving.'

So they went to say, 'How do you do?' to the other children, and then Bad Harry's mother said, 'I think we will have a few games now before tea – just until everyone has arrived.'

All the other children stood in a ring and Bad Harry's mother said, 'Ring O'Roses first, I think.' And all the nice party children said, 'Oh, we'd like that.'

But my naughty little sister said, 'No Ring O'Roses – nasty Ring O'Roses' – just like that, because she didn't like Ring O'Roses very much, and Bad Harry said, 'Silly game.' So Bad Harry and my naughty little sister stood and watched the others. The other children sang beautifully too. They sang:

> *Ring o'ring o'roses,*
> *A pocket full of posies –*
> *A-tishoo, a-tishoo, we all fall down.*

And they all fell down and laughed, but Harry and my naughty little sister didn't laugh. They got tired of watching and they went for a little walk. Do you know where they went to?

Yes. To the larder. To take another look at the spongy trifle. They climbed up on to the chairs to look at it really properly. It was very pretty.

'Ring o'ring o'roses' sang the good party children.

'Nice jelly-sweets,' said my naughty little sister. 'Nice silver balls,' and she looked at that terribly Bad Harry and he looked at her.

'Take one,' said that naughty boy, and my naughty little sister did take one, she took a red jelly-sweet from the top of the trifle;

and then Bad Harry took a green jelly-sweet; and then my naughty little sister took a yellow jelly-sweet and a silver ball, and then Bad Harry took three jelly-sweets, red, green and yellow, and six silver balls. One, two, three, four, five, six, and put them all in his mouth at once.

Now some of the creamy stuff had come off upon Bad Harry's fingers and he liked it very much, so he put his finger into the creamy stuff on the trifle, and took some of it off and ate it, and my naughty little sister ate some too. I'm sorry to have to tell you this, because I feel so ashamed of them, and expect you feel ashamed of them too.

I hope you aren't too shocked to hear any more? Because, do you know, those two bad children forgot all about the party and the nice children all singing 'Ring O'Roses'. They took a spoon each and scraped off the creamy stuff and ate it, and then they began to eat the nice spongy inside.

Bad Harry said, 'Now we've made the trifle look so untidy, no one else will want any, so we may as well eat it all up.' So they dug away into the spongy inside of the trifle and found lots of nice fruity bits inside. It was a very big trifle, but those greedy children ate and ate.

Then, just as they had nearly finished the whole big trifle, the 'Ring O'Roses'-ing stopped, and Bad Harry's mother called, 'Where are you two? We are ready for tea.'

Then my naughty little sister was very frightened. Because she knew she had been very naughty, and she looked at Bad Harry and *he* knew *he* had been very naughty, and they both felt terrible. Bad Harry had a creamy mess of trifle all over his face, and even in his real man's haircut, and my naughty little sister had made her new green party-dress all trifly – you know how it happens if you eat too quickly and greedily.

'It's tea-time,' said Bad Harry, and he looked at my naughty little sister, and my naughty little sister thought of the jellies and the cakes and the sandwiches, and all the other things, and she felt very full of trifle, and she said, 'Don't want any.'

And do you know what she did? Just as Bad Harry's mother came into the kitchen, my naughty little sister slipped out of the door, and ran and ran all the way home. It was a good thing our home was only down the street and no roads to cross, or I don't know what would have happened to her.

Bad Harry's mother was so cross when she saw the trifle, that she sent Bad Harry straight to bed, and he had to stay there and hear all the nice children enjoying themselves. I don't know what happened to him in the night, but I know that my naughty little sister wasn't at all a well girl, from having eaten so much trifle – and I also know that she doesn't like spongy trifle any more.

DOROTHY EDWARDS

PAUL'S TALE

' "*Ho! Ho!*" *said the King, slapping his fat thighs. "Methinks this youth shows promise." But at that moment the Court Magician stepped forward . . . What is the matter, Paul? Don't you like this story?*'

'Yes, I like it.'

'Then lie quiet, dear, and listen.'

'It was just a sort of stalk of a feather pushing itself up through the eiderdown.'

'Well, don't help it, dear, it's destructive. Where were we?' Aunt Isobel's short-sighted eyes searched down the page of the book; she looked comfortable and pink, rocking there in the firelight '. . . *stepped forward . . . You see the Court Magician knew that the witch had taken the magic music-box, and that Colin* . . . Paul, you aren't listening!'

'Yes, I am. I can hear.'

'Of course you can't hear – right under the bedclothes. What are you doing, dear?'

'I'm seeing what a hot-water bottle feels like.'

'Don't you know what a hot-water bottle feels like?'

'I know what it feels like to me. I don't know what it feels like to itself.'

'Well, shall I go on or not?'

136

'Yes, go on,' said Paul. He emerged from the bedclothes, his hair ruffled.

Aunt Isobel looked at him curiously. He was her godson; he had a bad feverish cold; his mother had gone to London. 'Does it tire you, dear, to be read to?' she said at last.

'No. But I like told stories better than read stories.'

Aunt Isobel got up and put some more coal on the fire. Then she looked at the clock. She sighed. 'Well, dear,' she said brightly, as she sat down once more on the rocking-chair. 'What sort of story would you like?' She unfolded her knitting.

'I'd like a real story.'

'How do you mean, dear?' Aunt Isobel began to cast on. The cord of her pince-nez, anchored to her bosom, rose and fell in gentle undulations.

Paul flung round on his back, staring at the ceiling. 'You know,' he said, 'quite real – so you know it must have happened.'

'Shall I tell you about Grace Darling?'

'No, tell me about a little man.'

'What sort of a little man?'

'A little man just as high – ' Paul's eyes searched the room '– as that candlestick on the mantelshelf, but without the candle.'

'But that's a very small candlestick. It's only about six inches.'

'Well, about that big.'

Aunt Isobel began knitting a few stitches. She was disappointed about the fairy story. She had been reading with so much expression, making a deep voice for the king, and a wicked oily voice for the Court Magician, and a fine cheerful boyish voice for Colin, the swineherd. A little man – what could she say about a little man? 'Ah!' she exclaimed suddenly, and laid down her knitting, smiling at Paul. 'Little men ... of course ...

'Well,' said Aunt Isobel, drawing in her breath. 'Once upon a time, there was a little, tiny man, and he was no bigger than that candlestick – there on the mantelshelf.'

Paul settled down, his cheek on his crook'd arm, his eyes on Aunt Isobel's face. The firelight flickered softly on the walls and ceiling.

'He was the sweetest little man you ever saw, and he wore a

little red jerkin and a dear little cap made out of a foxglove. His boots ...'

'He didn't have any,' said Paul.

Aunt Isobel looked startled. 'Yes,' she exclaimed. 'He had boots – little, pointed –'

'He didn't have any clothes,' contradicted Paul. 'He was bare.'

Aunt Isobel looked perturbed. 'But he would have been cold,' she pointed out.

'He had thick skin,' explained Paul. 'Like a twig.'

'Like a twig?'

'Yes. You know that sort of wrinkly, nubbly skin on a twig.'

Aunt Isobel knitted in silence for a second or two. She didn't like the little naked man nearly as much as the little clothed man: she was trying to get used to him. After a while she went on.

'He lived in a bluebell wood, among the roots of a dear old tree.

138

He had a dear little house, tunnelled out of the soft, loamy earth, with a bright blue front door.'

'Why didn't he live in it?' asked Paul.

'He did live in it, dear,' explained Aunt Isobel patiently.

'I thought he lived in the potting-shed.'

'In the potting-shed?'

'Well, perhaps he had two houses. Some people do. I wish I'd seen the one with the blue front door.'

'Did you see the one in the potting-shed?' asked Aunt Isobel, after a moment's silence.

'Not inside. Right inside. I'm too big. I just sort of saw into it with a flashlight.'

'And what was it like?' asked Aunt Isobel, in spite of herself.

'Well, it was clean – in a potting-shed sort of way. He'd made the furniture himself. The floor was just earth, but he'd trodden it down so that it was hard. It took him years.'

'Well, dear, you seem to know more about this little man than I do.'

Paul snuggled his head more comfortably against his elbow. He half closed his eyes. 'Go on,' he said dreamily.

Aunt Isobel glanced at him hesitatingly. How beautiful he looked, she thought, lying there in the firelight with one curled hand lying lightly on the counterpane. 'Well,' she went on, 'this little man had a little pipe made of straw.' She paused, rather pleased with this idea. 'A little hollow straw, through which he played jiggity little tunes. And to which he danced.' She hesitated. 'Among the bluebells,' she added. Really this was quite a pretty story. She knitted hard for a few seconds, breathing heavily, before the next bit would come. 'Now,' she continued brightly, in a changed, higher and more conversational voice, 'up in the tree, there lived a fairy.'

'In the tree?' asked Paul, incredulously.

'Yes,' said Aunt Isobel, 'in the tree.'

Paul raised his head. 'Do you know that for certain?'

'Well, Paul,' began Aunt Isobel. Then she added playfully, 'Well, I suppose I do.'

'Go on,' said Paul.

'Well, this fairy ...'

Paul raised his head again. 'Couldn't you go on about the little man?'

'But, dear, we've done the little man – how he lived in the roots, and played a pipe, and all that.'

'You didn't say about his hands and feet.'

'His hands and feet!'

'How sort of big his hands and feet looked, and how he could scuttle along. Like a rat,' Paul added.

'Like a rat!' exclaimed Aunt Isobel.

'And his voice. You didn't say anything about his voice.'

'What sort of a voice,' Aunt Isobel looked almost scared, 'did he have?'

'A croaky sort of voice. Like a frog. And he says "Will 'ee" and "Do 'ee".'

'Willy and Dooey ...' repeated Aunt Isobel.

'Instead of "Will you" and "Do you". You know.'

'Has he – got a Sussex accent?'

'Sort of. He isn't used to talking. He is the last one. He's been all alone, for years and years.'

'Did he –' Aunt Isobel swallowed. 'Did he tell you that?'

'Yes. He had an aunt and she died about fifteen years ago. But even when she was alive, he never spoke to her.'

'Why?' asked Aunt Isobel.

'He didn't like her,' said Paul.

There was silence. Paul stared dreamily into the fire. Aunt Isobel sat as if turned to stone, her hands idle in her lap. After a while, she cleared her throat.

'When did you first see this little man, Paul?'

'Oh, ages and ages ago. When did you?'

'I – Where did you find him?'

'Under the chicken house.'

'Did you – did you speak to him?'

Paul made a little snort. 'No. I just popped a tin over him.'

'You caught him!'

'Yes. There was an old, rusty chicken-food tin near. I just popped it over him.' Paul laughed. 'He scrabbled away inside. Then I popped an old kitchen plate that was there on top of the tin.'

Aunt Isobel sat staring at Paul. 'What – what did you do with him then?'

'I put him in a cake-tin, and made holes in the lid. I gave him a bit of bread and milk.'

'Didn't he – say anything?'

'Well, he was sort of croaking.'

'And then?'

'Well, I sort of forgot I had him.'

'You forgot!'

'I went fishing, you see. Then it was bedtime. And next day I didn't remember him. Then when I went to look for him, he was lying curled up at the bottom of the tin. He'd gone all soft. He just hung over my finger. All soft.'

Aunt Isobel's eyes protruded dully.

'What did you do then?'

'I gave him some cherry cordial in a fountain-pen filler.'

'That revived him?'

'Yes, that's when he began to talk. And he told me all about his aunt and everything. I harnessed him up, then, with a bit of string.'

'Oh, Paul,' exclaimed Aunt Isobel, 'how cruel.'

'Well, he'd have got away. It didn't hurt him. Then I tamed him.'

'How did you tame him?'

'Oh, how do you tame anything? With food mostly. Chips of gelatine and raw sago he liked best. Cheese, he liked. I'd take him out and let him go down rabbit holes and things, on the string. Then he would come back and tell me what was going on. I put him down all kinds of holes in trees and things.'

'Whatever for?'

'Just to know what was going on. I have all kinds of uses for him.'

'Why,' stammered Aunt Isobel, half rising from her chair, 'you haven't still got him, have you?'

Paul sat up on his elbows. 'Yes. I've got him. I'm going to keep him till I go to school. I'll need him at school like anything.'

'But it isn't – You wouldn't be allowed –' Aunt Isobel suddenly became extremely grave. 'Where is he now?'

'In the cake-tin.'

'Where is the cake-tin?'

'Over there. In the toy cupboard.'

Aunt Isobel looked fearfully across the shadowed room. She stood up. 'I am going to put the light on, and I shall take that cake-tin out into the garden.'

'It's raining,' Paul reminded her.

'I can't help that,' said Aunt Isobel. 'It is wrong and wicked to keep a little thing like that shut up in a cake-tin. I shall take it out on to the back porch and open the lid.'

'He can hear you,' said Paul.

'I don't care if he can hear me.' Aunt Isobel walked towards the door. 'I'm thinking of his good, as much as of anyone else's.' She switched on the light. 'Now, which was the cupboard?'

'That one, near the fireplace.'

The door was ajar. Timidly Aunt Isobel pulled it open with one finger. There stood the cake-tin amid a medley of torn cardboard, playing cards, pieces of jig-saw puzzle and an open paint box.

'What a mess, Paul!'

Nervously Aunt Isobel stared at the cake-tin and, falsely innocent, the British Royal Family stared back at her, painted brightly

on a background of Allied flags. The holes in the lid were narrow and wedge-shaped, made, no doubt, by the big blade of the best cutting-out scissors. Aunt Isobel drew in her breath sharply. 'If you weren't ill, I'd make you do this. I'd make you carry the tin out and watch you open the lid –' She hesitated as if unnerved by the stillness of the rain-darkened room and the sinister quiet within the cake-tin.

Then, bravely, she put out a hand. Paul watched her, absorbed, as she stretched forward the other one and, very gingerly, picked up the cake-tin. His eyes were dark and deep. He saw the lid was not quite on. He saw the corner, in contact with that ample bosom, rise. He saw the sharp edge catch the cord of Aunt Isobel's pince-nez and, fearing for her rimless glasses, he sat up in bed.

Aunt Isobel felt the tension, the pressure of the pince-nez on the bridge of her nose. A pull it was, a little steady pull as if a small dark claw, as wrinkled as a twig, had caught the hanging cord ...

'Look out!' cried Paul.

Loudly she shrieked and dropped the box. It bounced away and then lay still, gaping emptily on its side. In the horrid hush, they heard the measured plank-ing of the lid as it trundled off beneath the bed.

Paul broke the silence with a croupy cough.

'Did you see him?' he asked, hoarse but interested.

'No,' stammered Aunt Isobel, almost with a sob. 'I didn't. I didn't see him.'

'But you nearly did.'

Aunt Isobel sat down limply in the upholstered chair. Her hand wavered vaguely round her brow and her cheeks looked white and pendulous, as if deflated. 'Yes,' she

143

muttered, shivering slightly, 'Heaven help me – I nearly did.'

Paul gazed at her a moment longer. 'That's what I mean,' he said.

'What?' asked Aunt Isobel weakly, but as if she did not really care.

Paul lay down again. Gently, sleepily, he pressed his face into the pillow.

'About stories. Being real ...'

MARY NORTON

INDEX OF TITLES

Index of Authors

ACKNOWLEDGEMENTS

The editor and publishers gratefully acknowledge permission to reproduce copyright material in this book:

'Number Twelve' from *Tales for Telling* by Leila Berg, reprinted by permission of the author and of Methuen Children's Books; 'Goose Feathers' by Emma L. Brock, reprinted by permission of Thomas Crowell Inc.; 'The Clown Prince' by Malcolm Carrick, reprinted by permission of the author; 'Cold Feet' by Susan Eames, reprinted by permission of the author; 'My Naughty Little Sister at the Party' from *My Naughty Little Sister* by Dorothy Edwards, reprinted by permission of Methuen Children's Books; 'Did I Ever Tell You about the Time When I Bit a Boy Called Danny Payne?' by Iris Grender, reprinted by permission of Century Hutchinson Ltd; 'Elephant Big and Elephant Little' from *The Anita Hewett Animal Story Book* by Anita Hewett, reprinted by permission of The Bodley Head; 'Alpha Beta and Grandma Delta' by Meredith Hooper, reprinted by permission of the author; 'The Kidnapping of Lord Cockerel' by Jean Kenward, reprinted by permission of the author; 'J. Roodie' copyright © Robin Klein, 1984, reprinted by permission of Curtis Brown Ltd, London; 'Silly Billy' by Gladys Lees, reprinted by permission of the author; 'The White Dove' from *A Book of Witches* by Ruth Manning-Sanders, reprinted by permission of Methuen Children's Books; 'Paul's Tale' by Mary Norton, reprinted by permission of the Estate of Mary Norton; 'The Terribly Plain Princess' from *The Terribly Plain Princess* by Pamela Oldfield, reprinted by permission of Hodder & Stoughton Ltd; 'Dad's Lorry' by Phyllis Pearce, reprinted by permission of the author; 'Horrible Harry' by Diana Petersen, reprinted by permission of the author; 'The Runaway Shoes' by Edna Preston, reprinted by permission of Parents Magazine Press; ' Baba Yaga and the Little Girl with the Kind Heart' from

149

Old Peter's Russian Tales by Arthur Ransome, reprinted by permission of the Arthur Ransome Estate and Jonathan Cape Ltd; 'The Christmas Roast' from *The Silver Touch and Other Family Christmas Stories* by Margret Rettich, reprinted by permission of William Morrow & Co. Inc.; 'Elizabeth' from *The Silent Playmate* by Liesel Moak Skorpen, reprinted by permission of World's Work Ltd; 'The Practical Princess' from *The Practical Princess and Other Liberating Fairy Tales* by Jay Williams, copyright © 1978 by Jay Williams. Reprinted by permission of Scholastic Inc..

Every effort has been made to trace copyright holders, but in a few cases this has proved impossible. The editor and publishers apologize for these unwilling cases of copyright transgression and would like to hear from any copyright holders not acknowledged.

Also in Young Puffin

FANTASTIC MR FOX

Roald Dahl

Boggis, Bunce and Bean are just about the nastiest and meanest three farmers you could meet.

And they hate Mr Fox. They are determined to get him. So they lie in wait outside his hole, each one crouching behind a tree with his gun loaded, ready to shoot, starve, or dig him out. But clever, handsome Mr Fox has other plans!

THE Hodgeheg

Dick King-Smith

Max is a hedgehog who becomes a hodgeheg, who becomes a hero!

The hedgehog family of Number 5A are a happy bunch, but they dream of reaching the Park. Unfortunately, a very busy road lies between them and their goal and no one has found a way to cross it in safety. No one, that is, until the determined young Max decides to solve the problem once and for all...

Also in Young Puffin

MRS COCKLE'S CAT

Philippa Pearce

Peter Cockle longs and longs for a mouthful of fresh fish.

One of the things that Mrs Cockle's cat, Peter, loves most in the world is fresh fish for tea. One summer the weather is so bad that the fishermen can't take their boats out to sea. Peter has to do something about the lack of fresh fish...and Mrs Cockle is left all alone.

Also in Young Puffin

Milly-Molly-Mandy Stories

Joyce Lankester Brisley

Children love to read about this enchanting little country girl!

Milly-Molly-Mandy and her friends Susan and Billy Blunt live in a little village in the heart of the English countryside. They do all the sorts of things that country children enjoy – like blackberrying, gardening and going to the village fête.